Style Sisters

friends first

Liz Elwes

PICCADILLY PRESS • LONDON

To my parents – for everything.
To the fabulous writer Cathy Hopkins – whose amazing generosity
and kindness is legendary. I will be ever grateful.
To Giles Elwes and my children, William, Alice, Thomas and Jamie
for having such interesting lives and giving me so many lines
in the book (I hope you don't mind).
To my own style sisters: Frances Toynbee, Sarah Mower,
Jill Rothwell, Mary Saldanha, Marion Jeffrey, Anne Rands,
Rosie and Olivia McDonnell and Suzanne Vandevelde,
who I am privileged to call my friends.
To Brenda Gardner, Yasemin Uçar, Melissa Patey and everyone at
Piccadilly for their help, patience and guidance.
To Bernice Green who started it.

First published in Great Britain in 2006
by Piccadilly Press Ltd.,
5 Castle Road, London NW1 8PR
www.piccadillypress.co.uk

Text copyright © Liz Elwes, 2006

A catalogue record for this book is available from the British Library

ISBN: 978 1 85340 803 8 (trade paperback)

3 5 7 9 10 8 6 4

Printed and bound in Great Britain by CPI Bookmarque, Croydon
Cover design and text design by Simon Davis
Typeset by M Rules, London

Set in 11.5 Stone Serif

Chapter 1

Fact. I must have the softest hands in the country.

You need time and dedication to get them in this condition and I have now been in my room for days and days. The hours don't exactly fly by when you are lying on your bed, staring at the ceiling.

Depressed.

It was my keen survival instinct that made my trailing arm start patting tentatively under the bed. This produced a half-eaten packet of biscuits, so I ventured further with some exploratory sweeps of my arm and found an old magazine which had some excellent beauty tips in it – apparently sleeping with moisturised hands in gloves leads to velvety softness.

My Vaselined hands have barely been out of my woolly black school gloves since. Sadly the biscuits are finished. Quite a lot of crumbs have sort of woven themselves into the glove fibres over time but, overall, I would say it's been worth it. I could now, honestly, be a hand model. I can do all the moves. I could do diamond Tiffany bracelets. Or branch out and be a weather girl; I've got the required pointing skills and it would be easy for them to stick false nails on the bitten ones.

The other thing I found under the bed (and I don't want to brag but it was quite a haul) was this diary. This one that I am actually writing in now. My brother, Ned, gave it to me last Christmas. It is a blue and sparkly 'My Little Mermaid' Diary. I would almost have been touched by this present if I wasn't over six years old and if it hadn't been for the year before. And to think *he* complained about *my* present to him. How could lip balm *ever* be an unwelcome gift?

In spite of the dates not fitting the days of the week and it now being the end of March, I am going to start it anyway. I want to record my slow and painful road to recovery after Danny's sudden and devastating departure. It will all be very useful in our English lessons when we get going on the classics and dealing with Big Novelists. I will see how their made-up stuff shapes up against my own raw emotion. I can call upon what I write now in future essays and Mrs McGuy will say: 'Carrie Henderson, it is astounding how one so young can write about love with such maturity, clarity and simplicity. These other writers were practically dead before they knew enough to express these emotions!'

I will bow my head and bravely bite my lip as she cannot possibly understand what it was like when the first boy I ever kissed and my first *real* boyfriend (as in being allowed to tell people you're going out together and sitting next to each other on the bus) has had to leave my school and my life forever.

I won't write any more because I will start to cry again, though it's hard to tell if it's grief or hunger. After I said goodbye to Danny, Mum brought me up lots of cups of tea and toast and even a bowl of soup and a chicken sandwich on the first night. Heady days. I should have known she couldn't keep it up. It's not in her nature to be consistently kind for long periods. By the end of day two it was: 'Are you coming down, Carrie? It's shepherd's pie,' and wafting the mouth-watering smell up the stairs with a tea towel to torture me. I resisted. A broken heart cannot be mended by mere food. And now it's breakfast time and she's doing it again with the toast. It's obvious she's trying to starve me out.

I think it's something to do with her being a teacher; they can't sustain nurturing skills over an extended period. It gets trained out of them. (Miss Gooding practically cried when she first came to the school and I told her that a cat had given birth to two adorable fluffy kittens on my homework and I couldn't very well disturb her. Those were the days – now she'd laugh in my face or, I am sad to say, even use strong language.)

Mum's sure to be arrested when my skeleton is found in a corner of my room, though. I'm not sure how Dad, Max and Ned will cope with the prison visits. It's only a matter of time before she'll be rolling ciggies one-handed and yelling 'Got any snout?' across the visiting room to large tattooed women called Deirdre.

Right. To spare them all this fate, I am off to the kitchen now. If I am not greeted with joyous cries from my younger brother and a bit of sobbing into the old apron from Mum I will be offended.

Friday 9.45 a.m.

I am offended.

I do not wish to commit to paper the hurtful scene that has just occurred but I feel my therapist might find an accurate recording of events useful.

I do not actually have a therapist at the moment but I feel it's only a matter of time.

After washing my hair three times (which, by the way, ruined in ten minutes the melting softness of my hands and thus a future thriving career), I pulled on clean jeans and a T-shirt and descended to the bosom of my family. Well, half of it. Dad was at work and Max is on his gap year in South America.

I leaned against the door in a soulful way and breathed, 'Hi', trying not to make a dash for Ned's toast and cram it in my mouth. He must have sensed something because he drew his plate, and the dirty trainer on the table next to it, towards him. Disgusting.

'Carrie!' Mum was beaming at me. 'You do look lovely, *and* more cheerful.'

I looked at her and wished I could say the same about her. Not the cheerful bit, because she is, but she isn't exactly the last word in style. She was wearing an ancient T-shirt with a crumbly rock band logo on the front and comfy tracky-bums stretched over a not tiny bum. This look was finished off with dazzling white trainers. Truly, truly horrible. I won't say what she wears for school. Too much information. OK, a bit more – sometimes she cuts her own hair. It is very thick and frizzy. Enough said.

I was just sitting down and thinking that I should count myself lucky if my only criticism of my mum was her clothes sense, despite the starvation thing, when the next thing she says, apart from 'Do you want toast and tea, etc, etc.' is: 'I'm so glad to see that you've stopped moping around your room.'

Moping! What kind of word is that to describe my inner tragedy? *Three* days (nearly) I'd been in that room. I drooped over the kitchen table and tried to shovel the toast Mum had just handed me into my mouth in a depressed yet speedy way.

And then Ned said, 'You weren't that keen on Danny before you knew he was going away. You said that you thought he could be a bit boring.'

Don't younger brothers have such irritating squeaky voices?

'I never, *ever* said that!'

'You did.'

'Did not.'

'Did.'

'Did not.'

Etc, etc. Combine the voice thing with their uncanny ability to remember every single thing you have ever said, *even if you didn't mean it,* and it's really a wonder any of them ever make it to adulthood.

He opened his mouth again, but I raised my hand.

'Please don't try and talk to me about relationships, Ned. You are twelve. You love your skateboard and want me to be bridesmaid when you marry it.'

'Ooooh, I'm cracking up, Carrie. You should be in showbiz, you really should.'

I sighed.

It was obvious I was still way too emotionally vulnerable for all this. I had left my room too soon to cope with the outside world. Mum handed me some more toast.

'What's happened to Rani and Chloe?' she asked. 'It seems like ages since they came round. Why don't you give them a ring, Carrie?'

With quiet dignity I took the plate from her hand and left the room.

My therapist will be wringing her hands in sorrow at my insensitive treatment when she gets to that bit. (I've decided it's going to have to be a woman because a man might fall in love with the fascinating yet fragile personality which I will have developed by then. And I don't need added complications.) She will wonder what kind of extraordinary girl has the strength of personality to overcome that sort of childhood. In fact, she'll be begging to see me and I won't have to pay.

I have finished my toast. I am still hungry.

Now that I've been downstairs, the four walls of my room have lost their charm. Even the pink tree I painted on my wall with the tiny, stencilled gold leaves has lost its allure. On the branches I've nailed tiny tacks that I hang all my jewellery, belts and bits of ribbon, etc. on. I have rearranged this twice. Perhaps I do need to get out.

And Mum's last comment has hit home.

Before Danny's family moved (curse the promotional ladder in Pharmaceutical Sales) we had made the most of his final days by seeing each other whenever we could. I realise now that I hadn't seen anyone else. Not even Rani and Chloe, my best friends in the whole world. Danny had made it clear that he just didn't want them coming along when we went out and when he left I took to my room. Thinking about this is making my cheeks burn. I've just looked in the mirror so I know. Long blondy hair, blue eyes, unremarkable nose, burning cheeks. No wonder they'd stopped phoning. I have to face the painful truth: I have not been a good friend. In fact, I have been a pathetic, self-centred apology for a friend.

This is not a comfortable thought. What if I no longer have any friends? Rani and Chloe are the most loyal people in the world so you would not want to be the person who had failed them in the true and honourable friend department. Take it from me – we have HIGH STANDARDS as far as being friends go. High standards I suspect I have fallen well below.

I am overcome with shame.

I will make amends.

I will phone now.

Friday 10.25 a.m.

That's over.

I phoned Rani first.

'Hello?'

'Hi, Rani, it's me.'

'Who?'

'Me.'

'I'm trying to recognise your voice. Hold on . . . don't tell me . . . I've got a dim recollection. Did I know you in a past life?'

'It's me, the crappiest friend in crap-friends' town.'

'Ah-ha. Now that clears it up.'

'Rani, I am sooo sorry. I don't know what to say . . .'

'How about this: My once sharp brain has been taken over by mysterious boy power, which has robbed me of my senses. It has caused me to think like this: "Yes, lovely Danny, who I have known for three-and-a-half seconds, you are the most important thing in my life. You do not like Rani and Chloe, my dearest friends, who I have known since Miss Brown's Reception Class, therefore I will spurn them for your love . . .".'

'Ouch, ouch, OK . . . OK . . .'

'I haven't finished yet.'

'Oh God. Go on then.'

'"But now Danny, Boy Wonder, has gone to live in Birmingham

and I want my friends back because I am lonely and sad and I want to have a laugh again . . ."'

'Ooooh.'

'"Which is more than I ever did with Danny."'

'Double oooh.'

'OK, I've finished now. Where shall we meet?'

'Seriously, Rani? Do you mean it? That would be so, so, brilliant. I know I've been an idiot, but I swear, swear, swear, I will never be such a prat again. You know that I now realise that losing my friends would be the worst nightmare that could ever befall me.'

'Really? You always said doing a big poo in someone else's house and not being able to flush it down the loo was the worst thing that could ever befall you.'

'Yes, well, let's face it, that would be hell as well. And thank you for reminding me about that. God, it does seems like forever since I last saw you.'

'Well. Let me see, you went out with Danny for four weeks altogether. The last time I saw you was the last day of term, then the Easter holidays began. That was two weeks ago. Then Danny left and you've been in mourning for him ever . . . since now mmm . . . let me see . . . that would be for two and a bit days.'

'It's enough isn't it?'

'I think so.'

Huzzah! So now I'm meeting her in Barnaby's department store in town later. Rani says they are launching a new eyeshadow range in the beauty department. Her mum's a make-up artist and hears about these things. I also need a new PE kit as my old gym skirt is falling apart and my frontage has increased. Double Huzzah!

I have now done all these things since I phoned Rani:

1) Phoned Chloe. She was her usual calm and mature self. I honestly think she is incapable of a single mean word. You know in fairy tales when they say about princesses, 'She was as kind as she was beautiful'? Well, that's Chloe.

   She is looking after her brother, Jim, today. He's seven and has got Down's syndrome. He's very sweet and funny and I'm not just saying that because he's always irresistibly pleased to see me. Rani and I will see her tomorrow.

2) Tidied my room. I was like Mary Poppins with a little tweety bird on my finger. Personally, I always find scooping all clothes off the floor and chair and plonking them in the laundry basket a very effective start to any clearing up activity.

3) Changed into white cotton shirt and added big belt to jeans. Pulled on black suede ankle boots. Being a spinster is no excuse for letting one's standards drop.

4) Vowed solemnly in mirror and to this diary that I, Carrie Henderson, have learned a lesson and will, from this day forth:

   PUT MY FRIENDS FIRST

   (and will try to be a generally better person).

★ CARRIE'S TIP ● ● ● ● ● ● ● ● ● ● ● ● ● ● ● ● ● ●

Keep your jewellery from getting in a mess. Use a pin board (paint it a great colour first if you want to) and pin up all your bits and pieces. Thread rings through coloured ribbon and pin the ribbons to the board. You can also stick up photos, little pictures, fake flowers, anything you like.

Chapter 2

If I had known what was going to happen at Barnaby's department store I would have squeezed into my old gym kit for another term. You wouldn't imagine a trip with Mum to the schoolwear department would end in violence and me BEING PRACTICALLY IN FEAR OF MY LIFE, would you? But it did. Dr Jennings (for such is the sort of name my therapist will have) will be the on the edge of her big leather chair now, gnawing her pencil in anguish. She knew I wasn't ready to go out. But that's me all over, she'll be thinking. Plucky, plucky, plucky.

It all started so well. We picked Rani up and I was so pleased to see her grinning face looming up against the car window. She was crossing her eyes and had her tongue sticking out attractively. Her eyes are huge and hazel like her mum's. Her dad is Indian so she has gorgeous tawny skin too. She'd put her shiny black hair up in a ponytail and was eating a sandwich. She is always eating something. I think she lives in terror of starvation. It is very annoying because she is small and graceful and delicate looking. It is also unfair that she got boobs when she was about eleven. She can do cleavage. And here I am, fourteen years old and nearly six foot and thrilled because I've gone from 32A to 32B. Nature can be very cruel.

Rani thought she saw the girl first. She poked me in the arm to alert me, but *naturally* I had seen her. She was standing in front of us in the queue in schoolwear and chewing on a safety pin. It wasn't a huge one but if it had popped open her inner cheeks would have complained. The girl pushed it out every few seconds to make sure we'd noticed. We had. With one sweeping glance we had made one of our expert assessments:

Lots of hair extensions in black and purple.

Black lips and eyes.

White face.

Wannabe Goth meets Coco the Clown.

She was also not what you would call a slightly-built girl either if I'm going to be honest. She was wearing a huge, black, baggy garment that may or may not once have been a jumper and ripped leggings that disappeared into big workmen's boots.

Then this harassed looking woman next to her began jabbing her finger on a list on the counter, saying, 'Honey, it says here you *have* to have sports uniform.'

The safety pin poked out again. The kohl-rimmed eyes stared straight ahead.

'I know you're not happy about this, sweetie, but you have to have this stuff.'

The girl continued with the chewing and the staring.

'Now come on, we've been over this and . . .'

The girl whipped her head round to glare at her. A flailing hair extension barely missed my tender cheek. Rani and I shifted back a couple of inches.

'I'm not going to be *doing* any damn gym class, so I'm not going to need any of this, am I?' she exploded. 'I hate sport, Mom, you know that, so even having this conversation is RIDICULOUS!'

There followed a brief period of choking because it was difficult to shout 'RIDICULOUS' with an American accent and a safety pin in your mouth. But we were impressed that she tried.

Harassed Mom went in again. 'Please be reasonable . . . you know you have to do it.'

The girl took the safety pin out of her mouth and snarled through clenched teeth, 'I-won't-be-doing-any-sport.'

'I'm going to buy all the uniform anyway,' the woman replied briskly. You had to hand it to her. She had courage.

'Do what you like, I'm not trying it on because I'm never, ever, *ever* going to wear it. Don't you understand?! I never wanted to come to this stupid place in this stupid country and go to this stupid school.'

OK, OK. We got the point.

'What kind of dumb school makes girls wear divided skirts anyway? It's like the dark ages.'

Rani clutched my arm; I swiftly put the skirt I was carrying behind my back. I thought this might not be the best time to introduce the good news that we were at the same school.

'And what are you two Barbie dolls staring at?!' the girl hissed at us.

Well. Really! I'll admit that maybe Rani and I had outstayed our welcome in 'Eyeshadow World – Where Colour Talks'. The sales assistant had certainly thought so. But there was no need to be rude.

'Do they have Asian Barbie?' Rani whispered in my ear. I was still reeling at the girl's shocking accusation and opened my mouth to give a sharp and witty reply. Nothing had yet come out of it when Mum arrived panting at my side, flapping a fluorescent red gym shirt. Tragically that truly is the colour of Boughton High.

'Phew, good, you've not been served yet. Look, I got the last one.'

But then her eyes alighted on the identical colour in the pile of school uniform ahead of us. I prayed an internal prayer for it not to happen, but it was already too late. I could see the harassed woman looking at my shirt in Mum's hand and you could feel the womanly bond swelling between them. I caught safety-pin girl's eye and we looked at the floor and waited for the wave to break.

'Is your daughter going to Boughton High?' Mum opened communications.

'She sure is. She's going to be new this term.'

Oh, rub it in for her, why don't you? I almost felt sorry for her.

'We've come from the States, but I grew up in this area. My husband is going to come over and join us shortly. We've only been here a week trying to get Madeline . . .'

'MADDY!' The verbal explosion was deafening and swiftly followed by a Deathly Stare.

Her mother sighed, unmoved. 'Sorry honey, *Maddy*, ready for school.'

'Well, you must allow me to introduce myself . . .'

Please, please don't, my brain wailed. It was bad enough that Maddy/Madeline was already feeling less than enthusiastic about Boughton High. She really didn't need to know that my mum was the deputy head. But of course Mum told them anyway and even asked: 'And what year will your daughter be going into?'

'Year Nine.'

'Year Nine!' You'd think Mum had just been told she'd won the lottery.

'Well, Carrie and Rani are in the SAME year!'

Abso-bloody-lutely amazing.

'Where are you living?'

'The cutest village called Pitsford . . .' I felt Rani's grip on my arm tighten in anticipation. Don't say it, Mum. Just do not . . .

'Noooo . . .' Mum is practically swooning with ecstasy now. 'We live in the very next village, Moulton, don't we? Is Madeline taking the bus to school? It would be the same one as the girls!'

We drooped our heads as Maddy's mum said that she would.

'I'm sure that Madeline,' (I heard the girl's teeth grind), 'will love Boughton High. Carrie and Rani are very happy there, aren't you?'

We smiled wanly.

The woman beamed back.

'I think Madel . . . Maddy is feeling a bit nervous about starting school and meeting new friends.'

Was this woman mad? Did she have a death wish? Maddy's teeth-grinding went up a gear.

Ker-ching. Saved by the till. The receipt is handed over and even the bright smile on Maddy's mum's face dimmed momentarily. Yes, it is a small fortune for a pile of Day-Glo acrylic. Why the parents don't protest I don't know. It is a scandal.

At this point I thought it was over. They were on their way – bye bye, Maddy. *Ciao, sayonara.*

But no. I sensed Mum inhaling. She was going to say something more. This was bad.

'Would Madeline like to come . . .' she began.

Anyone could see that I had to do something. I gave Mum's shin a gentle warning nudge with my foot. Unfortunately it came out as more of a hard scrape and she yelped in pain.

'Carrie!' She was bent over rubbing her calf. 'What on earth did you do that for?'

And not only did I feel terrible because she was in real agony but, as I helped pick up her bag and the shirt, I also felt ashamed because I realised that Maddy knew what I'd done. I had seen the briefest ripple of hurt cross her face before she popped the safety pin back in her mouth and turned and walked off. Her mum gathered the mountains of bags and scurried after her into the crowds of shoppers. As she caught her up, Maddy turned and looked back at us, giving me a look of purest Death Ray contempt. It was at this point I realised I was in grave personal danger.

I wasn't alone in this thought. 'Do you think she's going to actually kill you when she sees you again?' asked Rani.

'It is a distinct possibility. Oh hell . . . I feel really crappy. This was supposed to my first day of being a better person.'

'But she called us Barbie dolls and was rude to her mum and just seems to be a walking nightmare. Why on earth would you want to spend more time with someone who behaves like that?'

But it didn't make me feel much better, because to be honest after all that time trying on the eyeshadow testers Maddy wasn't that far off with the Barbie jibe. Rani was blinking at me intently with one gold and one silver glitter eyelid. She had also tried on three lash-lengthening mascaras on top of each other. So had I. Glancing in the shop mirror, I realised that one deep plum and one lime green eyelid would have been quite enough without the rose blusher and the lip-gloss as well.

So what kind of day was that? Considering my resolution this morning to be a little friend to all the world, what have I achieved?

1) *Met a complete stranger who now hates me.*
2) *Attacked my own mother and caused her grievous bodily harm.*
3) *Made a half-hearted attempt at offending Ned with the skateboard jibe.*
    (I just put that in to cheer myself up.)

I'm making a mental note to do my very best to get Chloe on my side tomorrow about the Maddy thing. Problem. Chloe has a tendency to *see all sides* of an argument. And be thoughtful and forgiving (unlike Rani who makes her mind up one way – and that's that). Chloe will know the right thing to do and it'll have to be a better suggestion than Rani's, which was to sharpen all our pencils really pointy, just in case.

RANI'S TIP •
Before you put make-up on, decide what you want to emphasise - eyes, mouth or cheeks. Decide on one and avoid trying to play up everything or you will end up looking as overdone as that assistant at Barnaby's beauty counter, or us after too long playing with the testers.

Chapter 3

Saturday 9.10 a.m.

Chloe has just phoned. I told her everything that had happened. Again. I had already phoned her last night but I wanted to make *absolutely* sure that she was seeing it from the right angle.

We are having an emergency meeting in The Coffee Bean later today. On the agenda:

- *The Maddy Situation.*
- *The Lack of Boyfriend Situation. (Not Chloe's – she's been going out with Tom Mower for about a hundred years.) At Rani's insistence this is to include a brief discussion on her lack of snogging experience. Rani says she cannot count a brief kiss with her cousin's mate any longer. And he was six months younger than her. She says this just shows how desperation can lower your standards. She is looking out for another opportunity but she's going to be very fussy this time.*

When I called her, Chloe assured me, like she always does, that *'Everything will be just FINE.'*

'You are always so wise and calm,' I said. 'It must be because you are a woo-man of the world.'

'What *are* you on about, Carrie?'

'It can't be denied, Chloe. You started going out with Tom A WHOLE YEAR AGO. This means that you've had loads of snogging practice. It's no longer a big deal to you, is it? It's no longer an OBSESSION. You can get on with thinking about other things now, like developing a deep personality.'

'I don't think snogging experience has anything to do with maturity, Carrie,' she said. Which shows she's not right about everything.

'Anyway, Danny and you seemed to be having a snog-fest most times I saw you.'

'Yes, but it's not like snogging someone for a *year*, is it? I mean, after a year you could be in the Olympics doing the snogging equivalent of the triple somersault and backflip. You could write a book now I expect. Chapter One: Noses and Teeth – Clash Free Clinches. Chapter Two: Drool – Say So Long to Saliva.'

'Come on, Carrie, it's hardly rocket science. You just close your eyes . . .'

'Ah ha, but that's just it. *Do you?* What if you open them to have a peek and he does at the same time? What then, hey?' I was trying to blot out a particularly embarrassing moment with Danny.

'You could try gazing soulfully into his eyes . . .'

'Are you kidding!? I'm still working on Chapters One and Two. I need all my powers of concentration. I can't risk being distracted.'

'Maybe you haven't met the right boy yet.'

'What do you mean?'

'Erm . . . If you are with the right person you don't really worry about any of those things.'

Hmmm. Well *that* was food for thought. But I decided not to go down that road with her as it might end up with me having to admit that snogging Danny had not been the most thrilling experience of my life. Maybe it was the way he took a deep breath before he began, as if he was about to retrieve a coin from the bottom of the swimming pool.

I was hoping it could be better than that.

Dr Jennings and I both had our fingers crossed.

Saturday 9.30 a.m.

Rani has just phoned to discuss what we might do for Chloe on her forthcoming birthday. And to ask if it's OK with me if she tells Maddy that it was pure coincidence that we were in the same queue at Barnaby's. And that she's never really liked me. It's the threat of violence.

Ha ha. Very funny. I do wish the next meeting wasn't going to be on the bus though. It's quite a confined space for someone to resolve their issues with you. Especially when you already know that person is capable of being very aggressive and on the big side too. I think I could bear the shouting, but if it came to a fight she'd win hands down – my fighting experience being limited to giving Ned a slap round the back of the head when he nicks my ruler.

Saturday 9.45 a.m.

I must now pull out all my clothes because everyone knows that loads of people from school hang out in The Coffee Bean and you just never know who might be in there. And like I said, being boyfriendless is no excuse for letting yourself go. Mum always laughs and says she looked a sight when she first met Dad. Sadly no change there then.

Saturday 10.05 a.m.

Wearing: skinny blue jeans, blue T-shirt with brown cropped jacket and stringy brown leather belt. Have to wear black boots because I cannot persuade Mum how crucial it is to have the same boots in both black *and* brown. Found hair straighteners in Ned's room. Something to do with skateboard wax. Memo to self: *Get Ned back. But later.* I am off to The Coffee Bean.

Yippee!

★ CHLOE'S TIP •••••••••••••••••••

The condition of your clothes matters. Dirty collars and missing buttons are never a good look. Don't leave dirty clothes lying around – get them in the wash and remove stains and repair rips and holes straight away. Otherwise, on the day absolutely nothing else will do and you totally have to wear it, you won't be able to and it is sooo frustrating. The same goes for holes and ladders in tights. Always carry a spare pair (or if you are like Carrie, who walks into furniture all the time, two pairs).

Chapter 4

I cannot believe what happened this afternoon! I am on cloud nine hundred and ninety-nine. Dr Jennings will want detailed notes (it's so rare something this good happens in my life), so I'll reel back to arriving at The Coffee Bean with Rani.

(There was a Mum/holiday science project conversation first, which didn't go my way, so we had to meet up an hour later than planned, but I'm skipping that.)

We were just sitting down in front of two hot chocolates and chocolate chip muffins when Rani gripped my arm and gave me *a look*. There they were. Jonny Poynton and Chris Jones (or, to give him his full title: Chris Jones – School God). They are in Year Eleven and *très très* cool. Rani has had a minor crush on Jonny for ages but I don't see why myself. He's on the skinny side, has long strawberry blond (and I'm being kind here) hair, and vampire-pale skin. I think he looks a bit grubby but Rani says he looks dangerous. Yeah, dangerous like a weedy ferret. However, judging from the many broken hearts he leaves in his wake, what do I know? Rani harbours a fantasy that he will wake up and realise that she is the love of his life. Yeah, well so did the Little Mermaid and look what happened to her. Chris Jones on the other hand is all surfer-blond hair, and blue-green eyes set in a gorgeous, tanned face. He is lead singer in a band. Every girl in school wants to go out with him.

Rani had her back to them. She leaned forward and hissed, 'Is he looking?' I peered over her shoulder and was amazed to receive the widest, most devastating smile from Chris Jones. He was really and truly grinning straight at me.

'Well? Is he?'

Dragging my eyes away from Chris, I could see Jonny absorbed in his cappuccino and sporting an attractive frothy moustache.

'Not *exactly* at this moment.'

'What's he doing then?'

'He's just sort of staring into space.'

'Do you think he's seen us? Do you think he saw us come in?'

'Yes, I do.'

Oh my God. Chris Jones had just run his fingers through his hair and given me another big smile. I promised myself I wouldn't faint.

'I'm going up again to the counter. Watch this time and see if he looks.'

'Rani!' I was going to say something that she didn't want to hear, but I had promised that I would be a better person and so I bit my lip.

'Watch!' she hissed.

So I watched and it was difficult to keep my eye on Jonny with Chris Jones staring madly away at me, but I remembered my duty and kept my eye on the target. Not a flicker as Rani went by.

She returned with another chocolate muffin.

'Well?'

I shook my head and her face fell.

'I'm going up again.'

'No!' My hand shot out. 'No boy is worth the calorific content of three chocolate muffins . . .'

'You'll eat some too.'

'My point exactly.'

Luckily we were distracted, as was the whole coffee bar, by the entrance of a stunning, willowy girl. Her long, curly, dark brown hair was pulled back in a thin knotted strip of blue silk and she was wearing a short, white cotton minidress over her jeans. Pinned on to it was a green glass butterfly brooch, which exactly matched her eyes, and round her neck she had wound two or three delicate blue and green bead necklaces. She bought a coffee and, oblivious to the staring, came straight up to our table.

'Please go away, Chloe,' I said firmly, for it was she. 'I know now why I haven't seen you for ages. You are just too pretty to be my friend. Go and make some other people look plain and uninteresting.'

But she didn't care. She gave us both a big hug and sat down grinning. 'I have a plan about Maddy,' she said.

'You do?' Rani and I perked up.

'Yup. I have given the incident a lot of thought and I have decided you only have one option.'

'Which is . . .' Rani raised an eyebrow and made pencil-stabbing movements.

'Which is . . .' She took a sip of coffee. 'A Charm Offensive.' Chloe leaned back and looked pleased with herself.

'A What?' I can't deny I was disappointed with this suggestion. I had been hoping for something a bit more specific.

'A Charm Offensive! It means that you try to be incredibly nice to her. So nice that she can't resist it and realises how great you are.'

'You so obviously haven't met her, Chloe.' Rani sighed.

'Look,' Chloe continued. 'It must be hell being new and starting school when everyone else already knows each other. She's just frightened and defensive. It just made her a bit grumpy . . .'

'A bit grumpy! She's grumpy like Darth Vader is a bit grumpy!' I said.

'Being new is no excuse,' Rani chipped in. 'Jack Harper came into Year Eleven last term and he was friendly and normal right from the start.'

Chloe nodded. 'I know it wasn't easy for him after his mum ran off to live in France with that aristocrat. His dad, maybe because he's a self-made man, always felt that Jack shouldn't have gone to private school. That was what his mum wanted, not him. So when she left, he pulled Jack straight out. They were a very mismatched couple. She broke his heart.'

We both looked at Chloe, impressed.

'You get all the gossip since your mum became his dad's personal assistant, don't you?' I asked.

Chloe flushed modestly.

'But Jack's funny and interesting and she, she . . .' I knew this was sounding feeble. 'Was mean to her mum about not doing gym.'

'And she could do with the exercise,' Rani added.

'Girls! Can we have some positive thinking here, *please*?'

You see this is the thing about Chloe, she's *naturally* nice. She doesn't have to work at it. Or make resolutions to be a better person. Not that I'm bitter or anything; it's very hard sometimes for those of us who have to struggle with our dark sides.

'I am going to make a solemn vow,' I said.

'To do what?' Rani looked alarmed.

'I swear to befriend Maddy.' I swore in my gravest voice so Chloe could see I really meant it.

'I think I should warn you, Chloe,' Rani interrupted. 'Carrie has resolved to be a better person and do good deeds from this day forth.'

'Honestly?' It was Chloe's turn to looked startled. 'Is that wise?' Ha ha.

So we all agreed. Starting on the bus on Monday morning, I would commence The Charm Offensive (with Rani as back-up). The idea was that Chloe would step in as Plan B at school if all else failed.

We were just getting on to item number two on the agenda, which was very close to both my and Rani's hearts.

Rani had just asked, 'Should I ask *him* out?', Chloe and I had chorused 'NO!' and I had said at least she had more choice when it comes to boys because she was small and not a giant like me when there was a little 'Ahem'.

And Chris Jones was standing there beside our table, smiling down on us like a god from Mount Olympus.

This is so typical. Your concentration slips for one second and there you are shouting about being a boyfriendless giant in front of the best looking boy in the school. (This only ever happens to me by the way.)

'Hi girls,' he said. Looking completely at no one else except *moi, moi, moi.* I am in shock. I am trying not to melt clean off the plastic seating and flop under the table in a puddle.

'Having a party on Friday, be *really* great if you could come.'

I started nodding my head like a nodding dog in the back window of a car. Then I heard Chloe saying she couldn't go because she was going to her dad's for the weekend and I managed to squeak out a 'Thanks. I'd love to'. And Rani said OK.

'That's great,' he replied, still giving me a paint-strippingly-hot look. 'Look forward to seeing you.'

And he did a pointy clicky thing with his finger, swirled round and slouched out like a cowboy from a saloon bar.

Chloe and Rani start fanning me with napkins. Very droll.

'Tell me true, girls,' I blurted out. 'Is it not the case that the best looking boy in the whole school has just practically asked me out?'

'It is indeed true,' said Rani.

I couldn't help but notice that neither of them looks that thrilled for me.

'What's the matter with you two? He's a god.'

'He's not really my type.' Rani shrugged.

'Me neither,' chimed in Chloe.

'How can he not be your type?' I gasped, and Rani said that I should thank God that we don't fancy the same people because if we did one of us would have to kill the other one. And that would be sad. Chloe said that that wasn't a very enlightened or sisterly attitude and Rani politely asked her how she'd feel if she fancied Tom AND WANTED TO SNOG HIS FACE OFF. The idea of Rani with big, dependable Tom with his smiley face and big shock of unruly hair was so ludicrous that Chloe spluttered, snorted up her coffee the wrong way and sneezed it out of her nose. So the napkins had to come out again. It was just as well that Chris had left and wasn't witness to this spectacle of immaturity.

So there it is. I do feel slightly guilty about getting over Danny so quickly. I wonder if this makes me a shallow person? But I just feel deep in my heart that Dr Jennings would be urging me to move on and not *dwell*. The party seems so far away. Thank goodness. I've got so much to do before then to keep me busy. No dwelling time at all. Chloe's Charm Offensive has to be launched first. She's so confident it will go like a dream. We've arranged to go round to her place for a beautification session tomorrow but she also wants Rani and me to practise being charming. Cheek!

 CARRIE'S TIP •••••••••••••••••••••

A useful thing to do if you're lying round your room with some time spare is to dig out all your old magazines. Cut out anything you want to keep from them and stick them in scrapbooks. Cover each one with a collage e.g. cut up make-up adverts for beauty tips, clothes for style info, etc. Then you can take the unwanted magazines to the recycling bin and de-clutter your room.

Chapter 5

Another (!) brilliant day.

Rani and I went round to Chloe's. I got a huge hug from Jim when I arrived, panting a bit at the top of all those stairs to their flat. (Memo to self: *Must get fitter.*) The flat is very small – Chloe shares a bedroom with Jim and never complains. It always makes me feel very lucky to have my own private space in my own room. The thought of sharing with Ned makes me feel faint.

Charm Offensive Practice

Chloe got up from the little table in their kitchen where Jim was concentrating hard on his painting and put two of the kitchen chairs side by side. I sat on one. This was supposed to be the bus.

Chloe said she'd be Maddy, but Rani pointed out that she couldn't pretend to act like someone she'd never met. Chloe simply said she'd be the most sensible about acting Maddy's part and neither of us could argue with that.

Chloe went out and opened the kitchen door. 'This is me coming on the bus, OK?' I got into my role and smiled brightly. She flinched a little, saying, 'Try and look a bit more natural. Remember, I'll be very nervous. It's the first day of term in my new school.'

I gave another welcoming smile – she said it would have to do.

So I smiled, said, 'Would you like to sit here?' and patted the chair next to me.

And Chloe said, 'Why, thank you,' and sat down.

I continued. 'I think we might have got off on the wrong foot at Barnaby's. My name's Carrie. Would you like me to show you around school today?'

Chloe beamed. 'Yes, please,' she said, then folded her arms. 'There you go. What could be hard about that?'

Rani put down the crisps she was munching and said, 'Let me do it. I understand now. You want it to be realistic.' And went out of the room.

When she came in through the kitchen door I cooed, 'Would you like to sit here?' But before I could give the seat the tiniest pat she had leaped on top of me and had her hands around my throat yelling, 'Die, Barbie! Die!'

This knocked Jim's paint water off the table and on to his lap and Chloe had to go and get him some clean trousers while Rani ran around apologising and clearing up all the mess.

Then Jim got interested in pointing out the highlights of his Batman underpants and started shouting, 'I want my elf clothes. I don't want my yucky trousers!'

Chloe wrestled him to the ground a few times but gave up. He's little but he's strong.

'Where is the elf outfit?' I asked. 'I'll go and get it.'

'Stored with a load of the Christmas stuff in the attic,' she replied.

Now this was a surprise to me because I had no idea that they had an attic. She directed me to a door in the hall, which I had always thought was the broom cupboard, but behind a bucket and mop was a little staircase.

'Good luck,' she said. 'I hate going up there. It's filthy and there's an enormous spider that sits waiting for you and then leaps out. The Christmas stuff is behind the door.'

'Thank you *so* much.' I'm not terrified of spiders but I'm not that matey with them either. Not like Rani who loves all God's creatures, even lab rats and worms.

When I managed to push the door open at the top it was difficult to see at first, the window was so thick with dirt. I could see the bags behind the door. I scanned the cobwebby ceiling and swirly patterned carpet for the leaping spider. No sign.

As my eyes got used to the light I could see that this was more than a box room. It had beams across the ceiling and a small white fireplace. I guessed it had been a maid's room when the house was originally built, before the building was converted into flats. I could see some cupboards at the far end and I couldn't resist stepping carefully across the room to open one.

'AAAAARGH!'

The leaping spider hurled itself at me, ran over my hand and scuttled off into the skirting, chuckling to himself.

Rani was up the stairs in a flash. Not Chloe, I noticed. She knew full well what had happened.

Rani was not impressed by my ordeal. All she said was, 'Is that all? I thought it was the mad axe-man.' She looked around. 'Yuk! This room is icky. Let's grab the elf clothes . . .'

But I was getting the greatest idea.

'Rani!' I hissed. 'This could be such a great bedroom for Chloe.'

'Are you off your trolley! It's revolting and I don't think she would like our little eight-legged pal as her roomie.'

'Shh! Rani, be quiet, and listen to me. If we cleaned it all out, ripped out the carpet, painted the walls and floor white, it would look completely different. We could get some furniture. I know Mum is mucking out Max's room while he's away and she'll let us have some of his old stuff. We could make curtains . . . Oh come on, Rani, you must see what it would be like. We could do it for a birthday surprise!'

Rani said nothing for ages but just looked around. She eventually said, 'Well, you are the interior design expert. I'll help to get it done on time. We've got exactly two weeks.'

I gave her a massive hug, and jumped up and down with my hands over my mouth to stop shouting with excitement while Rani talked about asking Chloe's mum and making lists.

When we went downstairs I needed to hide my emotions and so I started up our favourite thing at the moment, which is being those women on telly who make people over. We naturally took the role of stars of the show, dishing out our advice to the needy. We always used people at school as subjects so there was an inexhaustible supply of need. I did Chloe's hair in four different styles while she painted Rani's nails and we discussed Jennifer Cooper in our class and how great she would look with a new hairstyle, etc. Rani has agreed to highlight my hair before the party. The winter months have dimmed its lustre and I want to look fabby for Chris's party.

Then we tried on all Chloe's clothes and didn't look anything like as good as she does in them, but we didn't care.

So another great day. This is what thinking of others does for you. I am feeling full of lovely thoughts of Chris *and* about Chloe's bedroom. Chloe's mum thought it was a lovely idea and asked if she could help. Chloe never goes up there, but she's going to keep it locked just in case. She'll say she doesn't want Jim going up there if Chloe does ask about it.

Anyway, tomorrow morning. My uniform is laid out on the chair. I have set the alarm for five-thirty a.m. in order to get myself looking as good as possible in case I see Mr Love Pants in school.

Let's hope the Maddy plan goes more like Chloe's version rather than Rani's. Fingers crossed.

RANI'S TIP ●

The right colour of blusher is the colour your cheeks are after you've been doing some gentle exercise. Run around the beauty counter a few times and get a friend to tell you what colour matches your cheeks. (Or you could climb up lots of stairs to someone's flat.)

Chapter 6

Monday 8.15 a.m.

The lovely, springy, dancing-inside feeling I had yesterday has been crushed to more of a shuffling-tap number. It is the first day of term and it's pouring with rain.

I am writing this on the bus. It is proving difficult. Rani is checking out the boys behind her in her make-up mirror and jogging my elbow. Chris and Jonny don't get our bus so I don't know who she's expecting to see. I mean, is she suddenly going to say, 'Ooh look, look who *is* that sitting on the back seat? Yes, yes indeed, it *is* Brad Pitt. For he has decided to further his education and, goodness me, he's chosen Boughton High. Well I never!'? But you try telling her that. She's forever the optimist in her quest to extend her snogging experience.

It was a pathetic scene at the bus stop. (Mum always leaves earlier than me, but on the first day of term, it's usually before dawn.) Sodden groups in the scarlet of Boughton High huddled together for warmth. My spirits only lifted on seeing Rani truck up carrying her new sports bag. She has begun to take self-defence lessons. Her dad is convinced that every boy who goes to our school is a dangerous sex-starved sexual predator (actually he's not far wrong). She has pulled off her usual trick of wearing mascara, blusher and foundation and making it look like she is wearing nothing at all. Unlike me, who has been up since the middle of the night and still hasn't succeeded with a look that is going to get me past our form teacher, Laser Eye McGuy. No make-up and I look like an albino rabbit. Especially having to wear this red monstrosity. (It's not all joy being a blonde, you know, but, having said that, I can't wait till Friday when Rani's going to put some stylish streaks in my hair.)

The reason I have brought this diary with me (don't worry, I have covered the little mermaid in plain paper) is that I was talking to Mum last night *casually* about therapy *in general*. (Best to prepare the ground as early as possible.) I know that I have bravely got over Danny, but I feel Dr Jennings wouldn't like me to give up on our sessions too hastily and I tremble to think what the next few years at school may hold in store for me. Mum told me that sometimes therapists make you write your dreams down and make interpretations. As I had to beautify myself for a possible sighting of Chris Jones I didn't have time to write down my dream.

IT IS VERY RUDE TO READ OTHER PEOPLE'S DIARIES WHEN PRETENDING TO LOOK AT SOMETHING INTERESTING OUT OF THE WINDOW.

And I think denying it sort of says everything there is to say. I rest my case M'lud.

Rani has got out her science book now and is pretending to read it.

She says she's not pretending.

I have just told her my dream and so I can now write it down IN PEACE. Yes, this means you, Rani.

So *those* are self-defence moves. Just a lot of poking and jabbing, if you ask me.

OK. OK. I will now admit it – if you stop – they can be quite effective.

Jet Barker and Melanie Green have just complained we are

jogging their seats. Jet has smudged her lipstick. Every day she gets on the bus with full slap on and then proceeds to get out her Chanel bag and trowels another load on top. The look is footballer's wife, but maybe not Premier League. This abuse of make-up offends Rani, the Maybelline Queen – YES, IT DOES – and it is all she can do not to wrestle Jet's lippy out of her red-taloned hands and chuck it out of the window.

Anyway. The dream. Writing it down will distract me until Maddy gets on at the Pitsford stop.

Luckily I am not at all nervous about it.

MY DREAM.

I am in Barnaby's with Mum and Chris Jones comes up and starts to talk to me. (It's definitely a dream because I'm not embarrassed at all.) He is asking me something, but I am distracted by an enormous Ronald McDonald that is floating like a balloon above us. He is coming closer and closer and I'm feeling frightened he might pop. By this time, Chris is putting on eyeshadow and Mum is saying, 'Shepherd's pie always is a popular choice, isn't it?' Then I woke up.

Pretty deep, huh? I mean where do you begin?

Rani is gathering her bags so I can ask Maddy to sit next to me.

She went all melodramatic, rolling her eyes and saying, 'May the Force be with you.' There was also some unnecessary strangling movements round her neck with her hands.

The bus has stopped. This is it.

Monday 9.25 a.m.

I think that I should start by saying, that in all honesty, it could have gone better.

Thank God it is now double geography (and there's a sentence I never thought I'd write). And thank God for those striking Cypriot baggage handlers who have left Miss Gooding and Miss Watkins stranded on the tarmac in Ayia Napa. We have been told by the supply teacher to 'Get on with your own work'. Translation: 'I'm not bothered what you do as long as you're quiet and I can continue reading my riveting Mills and Boon.'

So Jet is doing her nails on one side of me and Doug Brennan is doodling rubbish graffiti on the desk on the other.

And I can record the events of the morning so far.

When Maddy got on to the bus the noise died away and the only sound was spotty jaws dropping on red acrylic sweaters.

She was an extraordinary vision. Her hair was still in wild extensions and her round face was pasty pale against the matt black make-up on her eyes and mouth (what does Rani say? – *don't emphasise every feature*). She was wearing uniform, but unfortunately what we have to wear would make Kate Moss look chubby; on Maddy it was a seriously unflattering crisis. I was straining to catch her eye but Sasha Dooley was in front of her. Now she *is* one of the few girls who can look cool in anything. Even our school uniform. Her short, bobbed hair suits her heart-shaped face and her dark almond eyes always seem to be smiling at some private joke. She has this edgy look. Not that I'm jealous or anything. It's just you know she never trips over her own shoes in the street or walks round all day with a chocolate Rice-Krispie stain on her T-shirt. She is dead cool and no mistake and all the boys on the bus are gazing at her but to no avail. She prefers to hang out with guys who have left school and play in small, gritty local bands called Mouth and Murder. I think you could say that Sasha Dooley walks on the wild side.

I looked at Maddy again and called out, 'Hey! Maddy!' (As you would.)

She and Sasha both stopped and stared at me. Maddy's face flushed under her make-up, then went hard and angry-looking when she saw it was me.

But because I am fantastically brave (and didn't want to admit to Chloe that I'd bottled out), I was not daunted. I took a deep breath and said, 'Do you want to sit here?' And patted the empty seat next to me encouragingly. I ignored Rani across the aisle with her hands over her face.

Maddy looked at me as if I was The Creature from the Black Lagoon or something.

I patted the seat next to me again. (More feebly this time – for things weren't quite going like at Chloe's) and tried to give Maddy an encouraging smile. She looked confused. (Rani said later this wasn't surprising as my expression was a bit serial killer.) Maddy looked like she was thinking something through. Sasha, who was still hanging around enjoying the show, just stood there, grinning. Then her mates sitting at the back started yelling at her to come and sit down with them.

Sasha started waving and saying she was coming and Maddy began looking along the bus in the direction of the shouting.

Jet used the distraction to hiss at me from the back of my seat in her foghorn whisper. 'Who's your new friend? Surely it's the love child of Ozzy Osbourne and Ursula, the witch in *The Little Mermaid*?' And threw her head back and cackled loudly at her own wit.

Maddy then spun round and looked straight at me. She clearly thought *I* had been laughing. Before I could say a word to defend myself or explain she attacked. 'You think you're very funny, don't you? Do you think I want to sit next to a shallow, dumb idiot like you? Or your stupid friend?' She jerked her head in the direction of Rani, who had removed her hands and was now staring with eyes wide. 'You really think you are doing me a favour, don't you?'

We-ell. Had to admit she'd got a point there.

'You think I'm going to be thrilled that Miss Cheerleader has offered me a seat. Well, surprise. *I don't want it.* I had enough of bimbos like you in America. I know exactly what you're like and I don't want to know. OK?'

OK? Well, if you think that making someone feel like a pile of doggy poo is OK, then yes, I was. I looked over at Rani, who was looking indignant and like she might laugh all at the same time.

It was so unfair. So we had gone a bit over the top with the old eyeshadow that day at Barnaby's. It's not a crime, for heaven's sake. Now we're labelled Barbie Bimbos. Nothing could be further from the truth. I defy her to even know that Rani had any make-up on and could she not see the subtle tones of my grey eyeliner?

Secondly, how could anyone think that the rasping cackle that came out of Jet's mouth could be my laugh? I was outraged.

'Hel-loh?' The foghorn pipes were tuning up again. 'Quasimodo, go back to Notre Dame. You've got a nerve telling people that you don't like the way people look. Have you seen yourself in a mirror lately?'

'Shut up, Jet,' I said. Rani wasn't looking like she might laugh now.

'Someone phone the World Wide Fund for Nature and tell them to relax,' Jet said, grinning. 'The giant panda is alive and well and living in Pitsford.'

'SHUT UP, JET!' My voice echoed round the bus.

Jet opened her mouth to speak again but saw Rani's furious glare, pouted and sank back in her seat, sulking. The show was over and Sasha began – ABOUT BLOODY TIME – to move up the bus. Maddy followed her and I think that she was hoping to sit next to Sasha, but her friends had crowded in and she was left sitting next to an appalled Year Seven boy who plastered himself up against the window.

Rani had scooted back over to sit next to me.

'At least you tried, my brave little pal,' she said sympathetically.

I felt depressed.

'It's Plan B then,' she said, sighing.

'Looks like it. That was hideous. Damn my good resolutions and curse Chloe for her stupid Charm Offensive Plan.'

I then suggested that Rani, as back-up girl, go up and have another try at talking, but she said she felt Maddy had made her feelings clear and she actually still had so much to do with her life.

So Plan B it is.

It is Chloe's turn now.

★ CHLOE'S TIP • • • • • • • • • • • • • • • • •
Try something different. Go to the changing rooms with something you'd never normally think of wearing. Wear a colour you've never worn before. You'll never know what suits you unless you experiment. And it's OK to make mistakes sometimes. Though never wear Boughton High red acrylic – it's always a mistake.

Chapter 7

Monday 10.25 a.m.

The supply teacher has obviously got to a good bit in her book because she's wringing her hanky out. Jet has finished her fingernails and is plucking her eyebrows. What's left of them. She has just seen me looking and given me a nasty sneer. It is because this morning I won the class vote to be on the decorations committee for the school fund-raising dance. My mind is already racing with things like how many strings of fairy lights I can beg, steal, or borrow in the two weeks before the dance comes round – the day before Chloe's birthday. The dance is Mum's idea; she is obsessed with getting funds for a new theatre for the school.

I can see Rani in front of me really and truly reading a textbook and making notes though I doubt it's geography. She wants to be a vet. You have to be almost a genius to be one and as luck would have it she is. A bit bonkers, but a genius all the same. She has to work *très*, *très* hard though, all the time. She's top in everything. Oh my God, I've just had a really weird thought. Working really hard, being top of the class . . . do you think there's a connection? Surely not.

I am writing away and looking swotty behind a propped up copy of *Geography Today*. Heh heh.

Chloe is not here – she is still looking for Maddy.

As soon as we got in this morning we dashed to meet Chloe in the locker room. We told her what had happened. She sighed. She looked at us like a patient Border Collie might look at two giddy sheep it's having trouble with.

'You obviously weren't encouraging enough. I mean, were you really, really friendly?'

I looked at Rani in astonishment.

'Have you been listening to a word Carrie has said?' Rani squeaked.

'Yes. I have. And though you say that Jet is to blame, I can't believe that Maddy would have reacted the way she did just because she overheard somebody laughing on the bus.'

'Laughing AT HER, Chloe, AT HER,' Rani corrected. 'You weren't there, it was awful and she called us, she called us . . . *bimbos!*'

Chloe suddenly stuck her head in her locker and appeared to be urgently rummaging around for something, but we could see her back shaking.

'Are you *laughing*?' asked Rani.

After some more rummaging and a few snorts Chloe's face reappeared around her locker door. She clanged it firmly shut.

'No.'

'Good.'

Rani was looking suspiciously at Chloe's flushed but straight face. She turned as if to open her own locker and then whipped round to look again. But Chloe was ready for her. She stared back with her eyes wide and lips pressed firmly together. Rani held her gaze and then began to giggle and that set Chloe off in hysterics and then we all started rolling around the locker room.

'*What* are you doing?' said a sharp voice.

How swiftly the dark times return. It was Mrs McGuy, standing staring down from her craggy height with her hands on her tweedy hips. She probably spun that tweed herself in her beloved Scottish birthplace. Her short wiry hair matched the iron grey of her eyes which beamed unwaveringly on us. It was one of her medium-strength glares. Her full-beam glare is much stronger, I'm told, but then I believe that, if you actually see it, you die. This was mid-range stuff – just enough to have us all paralysed like rabbits in headlights. The fact we were all still standing proved she was merely toying with us.

She barked at us for making a disturbance and then barked at us again to ask if we had seen the new girl in school. But Maddy had apparently disappeared since she got off the bus – Chloe and Mrs McG hadn't seen her at all. And then Chloe went all bright-smiley and said, 'Please, please, Mrs McGuy, please let me go and find her. It must be so difficult to start school at this stage in the year,' (meaningful look), 'and I think it's our duty to make every effort to help.'

And she swung her bag over her shoulder, tossed her curls and pulled a face at Rani and me who were sticking our fingers down our throats behind Mrs McG's back. Off she went. Skippety-skip.

That was ages ago.

Monday 10.40 a.m.

Chloe and Maddy have just appeared. Maddy strode in all defiant and extension flicking and Chloe was behind her, looking at the floor and not catching my eye. The supply teacher, dragged away from the Honourable Henrietta's heaving bosom, was rendered speechless. This precious moment was broken by Laser Eye entering the room. Her face was thunder. Showtime.

Schlang! Schlang! Her lightsaber eyes assessed Maddy in a

nanosecond. Chloe scurried to the furthest empty seat, still avoiding my questioning gaze I noted.

'Madeline Velde. May I ask where you have been? You have missed registration and Chloe Simmonds therefore missed it too, searching for you. I assume you have a good explanation?' She looked at Maddy expectantly.

Maddy was leaning against the door and finding the ends of her hair extensions very interesting. 'I got lost,' she drawled, without looking up.

Mrs McGuy's nostrils went out on super-flare. 'You *are* Madeline Velde?'

'Nope.'

Hell. This was going to hurt. Everyone shifted forwards in their seats. I tried to continue writing quietly but my *Geography Today* kept falling over. Some of our textbooks are very poor quality.

'I beg your pardon?'

Maddy's eyes flicked up. 'My name is not *Madeline* Velde.' Her eyes then flicked over the rest of us to see our reaction.

'May I then enquire,' Mrs McG asked, her voice like the sound of icicles breaking, 'what your name is?'

'*Maddy* Velde.'

Run, Maddy. Run like the wind, while you still can.

'Really.' Mrs McG extracted the register very slowly from under her arm and carefully put a mark in it. I could hear the clock ticking.

'Well, *Madeline*, I do not know what the standards of behaviour or dress are in America, but I'm afraid what you are wearing is unacceptable attire for this school. I have no choice but to ask you to go and see Mrs Henderson who, I imagine, will have to send you home until you can return looking more appropriate. Jennifer

Cooper can take you to the office so that you don't get lost. We will be happy to see you again when your appearance meets school regulations. Goodbye.'

Maddy was looking defiant and for a thrilling moment we thought she'd gone completely bonkers and would risk saying something else, but Mrs McGuy's stare did its job and Maddy closed her mouth. The rest of us subsided like pricked balloons.

Jennifer, who is petite and blonde and as we know could be really pretty with a few style tips, made little squeaky noises and approached Maddy like she was a rabid dog. Maddy did sort of growl at her and they disappeared out through the door.

So that was it.

Maddy's first morning.

Could have gone better.

The lovely sound of the bell.

Now to catch Chloe and find out what happened with her and Maddy.

★ CARRIE'S TIP ● ● ● ● ● ● ● ● ● ● ● ● ● ● ● ● ● ●
Fairy lights can look great in your bedroom, as well as on Christmas trees and in school halls. You can put them around a mirror or hang them across the wall for a gentle glow.

Chapter 8

Monday 7.30 p.m.

It's a relief to be back in the sanctuary of my room.

Ned is spoiling the tranquillity a bit by crashing around downstairs looking for his skateboard. Ooh look – I can just see the end of it poking out from the top of my wardrobe. Goodness me. How could it *possibly* have got there? I'll give him another few minutes before I put him out of his misery.

I'm longing to know what happened when Maddy went to see Mum, but I know from experience it's not worth asking. Mum never tells me anything that happens in her office. She says it would be the height of unprofessionalism. I say it's just me showing a healthy interest in her work and should be encouraged.

I have done maths homework – which was extremely hard, had my revenge on Ned, eaten a Kit Kat and I'm having a little break before replacing the tatty covers on some exercise books. I need to pace myself to avoid burn out. It's been a day of mixed emotions.

I caught up with Chloe after the non-geography lesson but Rani got in there first. 'Well?' she said.

'Well what?' Chloe answered, all casual.

'Don't give me "Well what?"' Rani said. 'What happened? Did your superior Charm Offensive succeed where us lesser mortals failed? When are we going to be introduced to your new bezzy mate?'

Chloe looked vaguely up the corridor. 'Errm ... Is it maths now? We don't want to be late.'

'Hang on a minute, Chloe,' I said, gently but firmly taking her arm. 'Come on. What did you say to her?'

'Nothing much really. After I found her hiding in a stationery cupboard, I said how cool it must have been to live in the States and that I hoped she was going to enjoy Boughton.'

'Yes and ...' I encouraged.

'And would she like to meet up at break and I'd show her around.'

'And what did she say?' Rani asked.

'She said, well, um, she said that she would prefer not to meet up at break if it was all the same to me.'

'She never said that,' I hooted. 'Go on, what did she *really* say?'

'No, that's about the sum of it.' Chloe was looking intently for something at the bottom of her school bag.

'Never!' shrieked Rani. 'She never said that in a million years, we've met her, remember. Go on. Tell us the truth.'

Chloe flushed and looked pained. 'OK, OK. She said I was a do-gooding moron and go take a hike and take my pom-poms with me.'

Oh dear, dear, dear.

After Rani and I had wiped the tears from our eyes I looked at Chloe and sighed in a disappointed way. 'Well, you must have done something wrong.'

Rani nodded sadly. 'You obviously weren't encouraging enough.'

'I mean were you really, *really*, friendly?' I asked.

But by now Chloe was attacking me with her pencil case. (Did

I say she was a kind person? I must have been mad.)

'I'm not giving up you know,' I said.

'Quite right,' Chloe agreed.

'So it's Plan C then, is it?' asked Rani.

'Yes,' I said firmly.

'What is it?' asked Chloe.

'It'll come to me,' I assured her. 'For I have sworn a solemn vow.'

Plan C has not come to me yet so I will cover a book for now. I will start with English. Mrs McGuy was not impressed with the attractive doodles I scribbled all over the old cover and the thin paper I used before is falling to pieces anyway.

Monday 8.35 p.m.

Have covered *six* books in lovely green and pink striped paper from the present-wrapping drawer. I am now a tiny bit concerned owing to a vague memory that Mum bought it to wrap Gran's birthday present – a bedside table. I'll just stuff the left over bits in the bottom of my school bag. Perhaps Mum will forget she bought it. Now I have to make camouflage paper covers out of magazines found under the bed. Very time consuming.

Monday 9.20 p.m.

Finished at last.

Opened my wardrobe to start planning outfit for Chris's party on Friday. Did not see Chris in school today except from science lab window. I wanted to open it and say 'Hi' casually, but Rani and Chloe said as we were on the fourth floor it might not come out that way.

Have not mentioned the party to Mum yet. I have asked her to give me a lift in to school tomorrow. It means getting up early but I think that could be a good moment. This is my plan for how the conversation will go:

Me (casually): 'Mum, there's something everyone's going to on Friday night.' *Pause to give Mum time to mentally climb into her Gestapo uniform and to lace up her jackboots.*

Mum (in deceptively gentle tone – do not be lulled into false sense of security at this point; it is the fatal mistake of the amateur): 'What would that be, dear?'

Me: 'That really nice boy Chris Jones is having a few friends round. Lots of girls in our year are going. It's not ending late and his parents will be there.' *Not sure about all of this – but these are desperate times.*

Mum: 'Are Rani and Chloe going?' *This means: 'Do other parents think it's OK? I don't want all the responsibility if it turns out to be a drug-fuelled orgy.' Mentally she is stomping around in her boots and having a think. Not good. Time to work fast.*

Me: 'Chloe's going to her dad's but her mum* would *have let her go and Rani's mum is letting her go.' Not technically a lie because she is going to let her go. After she has heard that my mum has said yes.*

Mum: 'Well I suppose that's all right then. Of course you can go.'

Tar-rah! Well, that is The Plan anyway.

We were talking about the party at lunch today. Jack Harper was there. He's really good friends with Tom and we always sit with them. Jack's sort of tall and slim compared to Tom and though they both have dark hair, Jack's grows down over his collar and Tom's sticks up like an exclamation mark. Jack plays guitar in the band Chris sings in and writes their lyrics and he's pretty funny. Chloe was saying to him that she was torn between being sad she couldn't come with us and glad she was going to see her dad. Tom jumped in, a little too eagerly saying, 'You must, must see your dad.'(Because if she didn't we wouldn't be able to work on the room in secret.) Chloe looked surprised and then relaxed.

'You're right. It's not like Chris is going to notice if *I* come or not, is he?' And she gave me a special look.

Tom raised his eyebrows at this. 'OK, spill the beans. What *has* been going on?'

'Chris has Carrie next on his list.' Rani grinned.

Tom's face fell. 'God, Carrie, do you really like him?'

'Mmm . . . Maybe,' I replied.

'Why?'

'Ooh now, let me see . . . He's one of the best looking boys in the school, every girl wants to go out with him . . .'

There was background muttering at this.

'OK, OK, every girl *except* Rani and Chloe. He's lead singer in a band. He's super-confident. He surfs in summer.'

'*He surfs in summer!?*' Tom interrupted scornfully.

I mean what's wrong with that I ask you? Dr Jennings will be as puzzled by the general iffy attitude as I am. I suspect she'll diagnose a bit of the green-eyed monster. It is very sad when your friends fall prey to these negative feelings.

Anyway, Jack didn't offer his opinion, and I looked at him and thought: He really is a very good-looking boy, if you like the dark, intense look. He's been at school for a term now and hasn't asked anyone out. Maybe he was being quiet because *he* wasn't going out with anyone . . . And then I had this brilliant idea. I would find him a girlfriend! As part of my being a better person resolution.

What better person than me to be a girlfriend-finding-person? It is ridiculous he doesn't have one by now. I don't want to brag, but I consider myself a pretty good judge of character and believe I'm pretty sensitive to which people would go well together.

I have added this to my to-do list as a top priority. I am a glowing goddess of goodness.

Total failure of the Charm Offensive *is* a disappointment. But I will not give up on my mission to be a better person.

Rani has said she will help me with make-up in the toilets, as I am sure to bump into Mr Love Pants tomorrow and want to be prepared. I am practising my cool 'Hi' as I don't want to babble like an idiot, which, knowing me, could be a danger.

 RANI'S TIP ●

To get the no make-up look that Carrie needs for school, you need to have a good base to work with. Stray eyebrow hairs need to be plucked (pluck from the middle and underneath only). Then pat a light foundation underneath the eyes and on the nose and chin to balance out skin tone. Apply a neutral shadow on eyelids and a darker soft eyeliner on the top eyelids only. Finish off with mascara and a little blusher and lipstick in a natural colour. When pushed, a dot of lipstick rubbed into cheeks will work.

Chapter 9

Tuesday 6.30 p.m.

Party conversation – DISASTER. Did not go according to my brilliant plan at all.

After I had said my piece Mum smiled sweetly and said, 'Mmm. I'll think about it. I'll have to phone his mother to check the details.'

Obviously I now have no option but to find my passport and leave the country. How can Chris take me seriously after that phone call? He will suspect that I will want to play pass-the-parcel and eat jelly and ice cream the whole evening. I think I will die of shame.

This is the curse of having a mother who is deputy head in your school. She has the telephone numbers of everyone there at her fingertips. She's like M in the James Bond films. What chance of a normal childhood could I possibly have?

I know Dr Jennings would be appalled at the lack of trust. It crushes my self-esteem. I can feel it. Crushing away.

Maddy was not in school. She is not allowed back until she has got her appearance sorted and that mostly means her hair. She was off to the salon today. Melanie's mum works there and told Melanie. Apparently you cannot believe how long it takes to get hair extensions out. Cara Temple had some and she said moss was beginning to grow on her north side by the time they let her out of the hairdresser's.

I did see Maddy on the way into school though. I saw her from the car window, coming out of the flats at the end of Pitsford Lane. I thought they were derelict. I told Rani later at lunch.

'You see, it's another reason she might be so awkward. Perhaps she's really embarrassed about not having a lot of money,' I said.

'Her mum could afford to buy her all that uniform,' Rani pointed out.

'You can get grants,' I said, 'or maybe they just scrimped and saved every last penny. Maybe her dad isn't coming to England. They're just on their own. Struggling.'

Tom and Jack came over to our table to discuss Chloe's room makeover. Chloe does flute on Tuesdays and comes to lunch late, so it was the perfect opportunity to plan. I was also keeping my hawk-like eyes peeled for Chris Jones. Rani had worked her magic on my face and I have to say I was as far from albino rabbit as I possibly could be without tipping over even a tiny bit into Truly Scrumptious As a Doll. She is a marvel.

Jennifer was in front of me in the lunch queue and had obviously got over yesterday's trauma to the extent that she was feeling quite the heroine.

'She looked really outrageous, didn't she? She's a scary one.'

I was choosing between the healthy option and macaroni cheese, so I went 'Mmmm,' vaguely.

'You have to admire her nerve though. I often wish I had the confidence to do something different. I mean, not like that of course,' she said, laughing nervously, 'but just something a bit more stylish I suppose . . .'

This got my interest because I've had my eye on Jennifer Cooper for a while now. She's very pretty but never wears a scrap of make-up (even *outside* school) and just scrapes her hair back in a rubber band (very damaging to hair). She's got a good figure too. With the right clothes . . .

'. . . but I wouldn't know where to –' Her voice trailed off as she looked over my shoulder. Her head went down into the salad section and her little nose went bright red. I looked around but only found Jack standing there, proving that boys have the best deal uniform-wise: white shirt, black jacket and trousers. Even the skinny red tie looked cool. And what do we get? Acrylic jumpers.

'Hi you, how's it going?' I asked. 'Ready to plan operations for Chloe's birthday?'

'Hello, Jack,' Jennifer suddenly piped up.

'Oh hello, er . . .'

'Jennifer,' I assisted, deciding on the comfort of macaroni cheese – because of Mum saying she was going to phone Chris's mother.

'Yeah right, Jennifer. Hi,' he mumbled. He went on to ask me something but I never heard what it was because two hands clapped themselves over my eyes and someone shouted, 'Carrie Henderson! Gotcha!'

I screamed, jumped a mile in the air and, as I came in to land, my dinner tray hit something solid.

It was the chest of Chris Jones.

I watched in slow motion as my macaroni cheese slid across the tray and drooled over his shirt. Melanie and Jet, who were, naturally, behind me in the queue (will I never, *ever* get a break?) started sniggering, but I wasn't that bothered because I think there was a Year Seven at the back of the packed hall that had missed it.

So, so unfair. I'd been looking out for him *all* morning and the moment I dropped my guard I was ambushed.

Wouldn't it be great if the feeling of just wanting to curl up on the floor and moan to yourself instantly made you completely invisible? It would transform my life I can tell you.

I now harboured bitterness towards Mum *and* macaroni cheese.

The dinner lady chucked him some kitchen roll. With a look of revulsion he wiped off his shirt and then handed me the tissues. Jack had disappeared.

'I'm sorry,' I said. What else could I say?

'Nah, that's OK,' he replied, in a not-very-convinced tone. Then he gave himself a sort of shake to regain his composure and forced his features into a smile. You could see it was an effort.

Then he said the magical words. 'You still coming Friday, then?'

In excitement I clenched my fingers. I felt the macaroni cheese squidging through them. 'Yeah sure.' (I will probably have to run away from home and end up in care but it will be worth it.)

'Brilliant.' He pointed his finger at me and made a clicking noise. 'See ya.'

So that is my faithful recording of that bit. But the events in the lunch queue were not over.

'He's just gorgeous, isn't he?' sighed this voice at my side and I looked down to see Jennifer looking all dreamy.

'I know,' I agreed, trying to find some clean kitchen roll to wipe my hands on. 'I just love that streaky blond hair.'

'Blond!? Jack Harper's not blond!'

'Jack? Jack! Sorry. I thought you were talking about Chris.'

'Chris! You're joking? Our parents are best friends. I've known him since I was two. No. Jack Harper. He's so, so poetic-looking and handsome.'

'Seriously? You really like Jack?'

'God. Do you think he noticed I fancy him?'

'No.' I shook my head and said honestly, 'I do not think he did.'

'He's way out of my league anyway. Boys just don't seem to see me as girlfriend material.'

I thought of the way Nathan Ryan looks at her across the classroom and wondered if she was right about that. But she liked Jack. That was very interesting news to me. I felt A Plan creaking into motion.

'Perhaps you should try doing something a bit different so they start seeing you in a new way.'

'Like what?'

'Like a new hair style, or make-up, or different clothes.' (Oooh dear. Was that a bit much all at once?)

'I wouldn't know where to start. I try and then I just get it so wrong and look a fool.'

'I'd help you out.'

At last. A double opportunity to be a better person. I would be helping Jennifer *and* Jack. Chloe and Rani would be proud of me. Surely they would want to help too?

'Chloe and Rani would want to help too,' I said.

'Are you *serious*?'

'Sure.' I was a glowing goddess of goodness yet again.

'Could you do it before Chris's party? His mum made him invite me and I know that Jack's going to be there.'

'Sure,' I said. 'Come over after school on Friday.'

In the current circumstances this was an optimistic invitation. But what the hell.

I was distracted by Tom waving his arms and mouthing 'Hurry up', so I said bye and went to sit down.

'Do you always chuck food over the people you fancy?' he asked, smugly.

'Ha ha.'

Then Jack suddenly got very official sounding. 'Hadn't we better be getting on with it?'

There was that moodiness again, but don't worry, Jack! Your single days are nearly over. Thanks to me.

Tuesday 7.05 p.m.

Mum has just come in (short-sleeved floral shirt, maroon elasticated -waist skirt) to let me know that she has phoned Chris's mother. She spoke to his sister. His mum is away till Thursday at her aunt's. Mum has left a message with her that she will call again. He will never, ever speak to me again now he knows I am treated like a five-year-old. How much humiliation can one girl bear? Pass me the Jelly Babies.

Tuesday 7.35 p.m.

I have made myself a plate of pasta. I acted silent and hurt with Mum in the kitchen. I would like to act furious and ranting but daren't risk blowing the slim chance I may still have of having permission to go to the party. Rani has told her mum that mine has said yes. There is so much at stake. I have to go to that party. I need the snogging experience.

When you want to find something special (for a big party, for instance) it doesn't necessarily mean spending a lot on a brand new outfit. Trawl the charity shops for second-hand clothes. Always go for good quality items and check the fabric for stains and holes. Then, glam them up! It is amazing what you can do with bits of ribbon, beads or lace. And you can alter sleeve lengths and hemlines too.

Chapter 10

Wednesday 8.00 p.m.

Maddy came back today.

Jet had caught a glimpse of her going into Mum's office and she waylaid me by the lockers, gasping with excitement. 'Your new best friend "freak-girl" is back. Oh my God! You have just got to see her. You won't believe it. Can't stop. Got more people to tell.' And she was off.

Maddy didn't appear for registration and then we had games. I was sitting on the bench in the changing room, with my legs stuck out: it was a depressing sight.

I want bony knees and ankles. I want people to say, 'She's got legs like a racehorse,' not, 'She's got legs like the bendy tubes they give you to play with at the swimming pool.' Even deep thinkers can be shallow sometimes.

Rani was plaiting her hair and Chloe was putting on some lip balm (you see, it's like I told Ned – always useful) when Maddy appeared at the door with my mum behind her.

You would not have recognised her. All the make-up had been scrubbed off exposing a pale, dull complexion. Her blue eyes were red-rimmed. She had obviously been crying.

Her thick, dyed-black hair was now shorter, with a centre parting (there are few people who can get away with one of those and Maddy isn't one of them) and the hair now came to just above her shoulders. She blew her swollen red nose on a tissue and stood completely still, as if waiting for all of us to take it in.

Mum must have let her change in the office because she was already in gym gear. The clothes she had sworn she would never wear. She looked very vulnerable and alone. I actually wanted to go up and give her a big hug.

Mum looked around the room. 'Sasha, it's Maddy's first PE lesson, could she walk with you to the sports field please?'

Sasha gave a non-committal shrug and Maddy gave her a look, which was a combination of admiration and trying to appear that she couldn't care less. Sasha didn't notice.

Miss Baxter clapped her hands and yelled, 'To the field, everyone.'

A groan went up because it was freezing and wet outside. A mean grey sky hung over the winnowing plains of the sports field and an icy wind whipped my legs up into mottled red perfection. Miss Baxter herded us along. (I'm putting all this in so Dr Jennings can get some idea of how harsh school life is.) All we needed were some tattered shawls to wrap around our frail frames and we would look just like a string of starving peasants, off to the fields, to dig in the iron-hard earth for mouldy potatoes.

Miss Baxter was yelling in hearty tones, 'Come on, girls, it's early spring in England, not winter in Siberia. Stop complaining.'

Rani, Chloe and I fell in behind Sasha and her mate Tess. Maddy was tagging alongside them. So much for looking after her. Tess was hopping around Sasha like a court jester. 'It was a good gig last night. Wayne had way, way too much, didn't he?

Sasha gave a smile but said nothing.

Tess tried again. 'And then he flushed his fags down the toilet by accident. He was *so* mad.'

Sasha looked up at the rain.

Tess continued gamely. 'I could do with a fag now instead of running round the freaking field in the freaking rain.'

Sasha turned slowly to look at her, surprised. 'You haven't got any *here*, have you?'

'I've got two in my pocket. And a lighter.'

Sasha raised her eyebrows.

'Thought I could sneak off to the wood,' Tess said boldly, 'but it's not going to happen. Baxter's got her eye on us and it's pissing with rain anyway.'

'I'll have one,' a voice said. It was Maddy.

They had forgotten she was there.

'What?' Tess sneered.

'I'll have one. If you could spare one. I'm, er, gasping.'

'You smoke?' Sasha was looking at her doubtfully.

'Sure, all the time. And drink. In the States we had some really wild parties.'

Rani gave me a 'Yeah, sure you did' look.

Before anyone could say anything else Miss Baxter was setting us all off running around the field. Jet and Sasha shot off because they are as speedy as anything. The rest of us broke into a lumbering trot like a herd of mildly startled cows.

The rain just kept coming down and in the end even Miss Baxter had to admit defeat.

'About time,' dripped Rani. 'One more minute and I was going to call Child Line.'

'Oh my God. I don't believe it,' Chloe gasped.

We thought it was an overreaction until we realised that she was talking about the sight of Tess handing something over to Maddy.

'She's only doing it to impress them.' I groaned. 'I don't believe she knows one end of a cig from the other. If she doesn't come in now Miss Baxter will go mental.'

Maddy had now slipped away from the group and was heading for the woods. Or the clump of trees at the side of the playing field that we call the woods. Sasha and Tess watched her go, shrugged their shoulders and walked towards the changing rooms.

'Look,' I said. 'I have a plan. You go and distract Miss Baxter and I'll go and get her.'

Chloe and Rani looked doubtful but I hurtled off. I would show them that I meant it when I said I was going to try to be a better person.

When I pushed away the dripping branches I saw Maddy with the cigarette in her mouth, sadly flicking the lighter switch, over and over, in vain.

'It's too wet,' I said, walking towards her. 'Come back in. It's just not worth it.'

She jumped at my voice and then saw me. Her shoulders slumped in relief.

'God, it's you. What is it with you? Why can't you just leave me alone?'

'Because I don't want you to get into trouble for something this stupid. You're not impressing anyone.'

She backed away.

'Go away.' She flicked the lighter again.

She really was a very exasperating person at times. Even if she did have a deprived home life, it would be no excuse for this scenario. And I was putting myself on the line for her.

'No. I won't go away until you come with me.'

'Well, I'm not going to. Take a hike,' she said, focussing on the lighter again.

Now I was actually getting very damp and cross. Which is sort of an excuse for everything that happened next.

I took another step towards her. 'Come on. We're going in.'

'Oh yeah, you gonna make me?' She drew herself up. One thing was for sure, in spite of my height, physical force was not an option. She looked pretty solid standing there.

That is when I can only describe a red mist of frustration coming down upon me. I must have been just overwhelmed with exasperation and irritation, because my arms raised themselves into the air above my head and my hands made themselves into claw shapes and I wouldn't like to swear on it but I think I started to make snarling noises.

Look. I was *desperate*, OK?

Her eyes widened and she backed away a bit more into the trees behind her. I began to growl some more and jog slowly towards her.

'Go away!' she yelled. But I kept going with the bear impression. I snarled again.

'You're crazy, you know that!' she yelled, before throwing down the lighter and ciggie on to the mud and breaking into a run. I chased her. I chased her clean out of the woods and across the field.

Rani and Chloe said it was hard to do the scene full justice in words. They had been engaging Miss Baxter in an interesting discussion about netball rules to keep her with her back to the woods when Maddy had burst out of the trees followed closely by a tall girl with waving arms.

They had then watched in silence as I tripped on the slippery grass and went sprawling into one of the numerous puddles appearing all over the field. Chloe said that the good thing that came out of it all was that Maddy, so miserable at the start of the day, had really cheered up at that point.

Hoo-ray.

By the time I had staggered over to them Miss Baxter looked like she would explode but Maddy was saying, 'I lost my bearings because it's my first PE lesson. Carrie came to find me.'

Miss Baxter raised her eyebrows at me.

'And there was a bee in the wood. It was after us and, and . . .' I added desperately.

Her eyebrows disappeared into her hairline.

'. . . I thought it might be a killer bee,' I finished, quietly.

A huge clap of thunder saved me from certain death and then the rain became torrential, so Miss B lost heart, exhaled, and said, 'Go in and don't let it happen again. Carrie get cleaned up.'

And that would have been the end of it, except, as we were trudging back into school, Chloe and Rani suddenly started walking quickly on either side of me. 'Carrie, keep your eyes straight ahead, OK? Just keep going towards the door,' Chloe said.

'Whatever you do, don't look right,' Rani added.

So of course I looked right and there was Chris, Jonny, Jack and Tom all heading off to some lesson. Chloe gave Tom a warning look and we glided by silently as they stood there. They made no comment but I thought their expressions looked strained.

'Do I look truly hideous?' I sighed after we had passed them.

'Noo, nooo,' Chloe said, soothingly. But then I got inside and saw myself in the mirror, I know they had lied. My hair lay plastered over one side of my face, dripping plops of dirty water on the changing room floor. On the exposed side of my face, from behind a thick black mask of mud, a little bright eye blinked back at me. Casting this eye downwards I could see splodges on my legs, accentuating perfectly their pale quality. And when I opened my mouth to exclaim in horror, I saw grass stuck on my teeth – placing the icing on the cake of the overall look. Which was mad, old hag. Well, I thought, just let me die now. I might as well – I have no future. Chris will never, ever consider me as his girlfriend now he's seen me like this.

So that was it. I have one hundred per cent had enough of trying to help Maddy Velde. Let her try and keep up with Sasha and her mates and see where that gets her. She is officially crossed off my to-do list. With indelible black marker. She is on her own now.

CARRIE'S TIP •

Make your bathroom a beauty spa. Clear and sort all the bottles and potions. Then get some clean towels, light a scented candle (if your mum will let you) and put a face mask on. This will unclog your pores (of mud or anything else lurking there) and de-stress you at the same time.

Chapter 11

I am worried that I am going mad. Chloe and Rani told me it was nonsense, and that I was just in a *very* stressful situation and my instincts took over – anyone might have started growling and chasing someone out of the woods.

Hmm.

What if *I am* a lunatic doomed to spend all my days locked in an attic, while some hussy called Jane Eyre runs about downstairs trying to get off with my husband? What if everyone else already knows that I am mad? And I'm the only one who isn't aware that I am as nutty as a fruitcake?

Sadly this is not just because of the woods incident, although I do think about this quite a lot. But Rani says she does too, which I find comforting.

Unless of course we are both mad. It's quite possible. And Chloe is our minder . . .

I'm going to stop writing about this now because it's freaking me out.

Chloe phoned and said I must not give up on Maddy and rub her off my list with indelible black pen. She felt that, as I staggered across the field towards them, she sensed a shift in Maddy's attitude.

'Yes, I saw that change in attitude,' I responded sarcastically. 'It seemed to be a doubled over, holding one's sides going ha ha ha sort of attitude from where I was standing.'

But she said she thinks Maddy appreciated what I did in a

weird way. However, Maddy is still stalking Sasha, trying to impress her. She's going to Chris's party with them on the promise she brings booze with her. I heard her bragging on the bus about what a wild time she intends to have. Chloe has persuaded me to continue to be friendly and not to poke her with pencils when I next see her. She said Maddy didn't ask me to come and find her in the woods. Which is true. And she didn't tell Miss Baxter that I chased her. Which is also true.

I feel better not giving up. Especially so soon after I'd decided to try harder to be a better person.

But I am pushed to the limit. What with the macaroni and the mud, I'm clinging on to my chances of getting off with Chris Jones by my bitten fingernails. I will need to look like the babe of babes on Friday night.

Which reminds me. I bought the hair bleach from the chemist today. I can't wait to lighten my hair. I'm going for a summer sun-kissed look. I know Rani said she would help me do highlights before the party on Friday, but I want cheer myself up with some beautification *now*. I cannot live with my dull locks a moment longer. How hard can it be? If I ever get permission to go to this party I want Chris Jones to go weak when he sees me. I am going to the bathroom to mix up the paste. I have put on the plastic gloves like Rani told me to – you do not want peroxide on your fingers. It's very harsh stuff and not good for your skin. I do not want all that hard work with the Vaseline and gloves to be ruined.

Thursday 6.50 p.m.

I am going to phone Rani now. To be truthful, it is not as easy as I imagined to do your own highlights. You have a mascara wand thingy and it's hard to keep the bits you have done away from the bits you haven't, plus, it's all rather drippy. There was also a diagram about dyeing it in two stages if you have long hair which I couldn't quite work out. I will clear up the mess in the bathroom when I rinse it out. It is very boring waiting. I have flicked through a magazine and also keep trying to work out the instructions. How long you leave it in seems to depend on what colour your hair is to start with and I'm not quite sure if I'm Ash Blonde, Dark Blonde or Beige Blonde so I need to ask her advice on this. I also need to tell her about My Very Exciting New Plan to find a girlfriend for Jack, soon to be Our Very Exciting New Plan.

Thursday 7.20 p.m.

I totally blame Rani. If she had just said, 'Yes, that sounds a great idea,' everything would have been all right. But no.

'Jennifer Cooper!' she screeched.

'No need to yell,' I replied. I had to pull the phone away from my ear to not be deafened.

And then she said it again. Just as shrieky. 'Jennifer Cooper!'

'What's wrong with that?' I said. 'You like her, don't you?'

'Yes, of course I like her, but what makes you think for one teeny-weeny minute that Jack might like her?'

'Why not? She's clever and sort of intense. And so's he.'

'Mmmm, yes,' she replied. 'So far perfectly logical. But call me crazy, couldn't the little hitch in your otherwise flawless plan be that he has never, ever shown the slightest bit of interest in her?'

So I said, 'That is where we come in.'

She said, 'We?' suspiciously.

'Yes WE. I spoke to Jennifer yesterday and she is mad, mad, mad for Jack. She just lacks confidence and so he doesn't notice her.'

I took a deep breath and crossed my fingers.

'I said that we would give her a makeover before Chris's party.'

Phone away from ear again. When I put it back I said, 'I have to say that I am a bit disappointed with your negative tone.'

'I'm feeling a bit disappointed that you've gone bonkers.'

So I went for the final push. 'Come on, trust me on this one. I really do believe that she could look so pretty. We've talked about it so many times. She *wants* us to do it. Jack would be bound to notice the difference and then she would have the confidence to talk to him and then TRA-LAH! Romance.'

I even bleached a spot on my school shirt because I was so excited. But Rani wasn't.

'Carrie, I'm not at all sure about this and I don't think Chloe will be. I think it's got doomed written all over it.'

'But why oh why? Why shouldn't Jack like the lovely made-over Jennifer? And Chloe will be fine about it because she is a very *kind* and *giving* person.'

'Oh, no,' she said. 'You're not pulling that one on me.'

'Yup, very kind and very thoughtful is Chloe. She'd *always* want to help a friend in need.'

'OK, OK.'

(Huzzah! Success!)

'Look. I don't have a major problem with doing Jennifer's hair and make-up for the party, but listen to me, Carrie, this is important. The Jack thing is a no-no.'

'*Why*? I can't see what's wrong with it.'

'Apart from the fact that I have already told you loud and clear that Jack doesn't fancy Jennifer?'

So I said, 'Well, how do you really and truly know that, Rani? I mean how can you tell that when he sees her all dressed up, he won't say "Wow!" and love will not bloom?'

'Your turn to trust me, Carrie. I just know that if he's interested in anyone it's definitely not Jennifer Cooper. I hope that you haven't given her any big hopes about Jack?'

'Absolutely not.' I felt a bit shifty. 'Well, not specifically.'

'What does that mean?'

Honestly, sometimes she's worse than my mother. (Who still hasn't let me know if I can go to this party anyway.) Definitely time to change the subject. So I asked her how long you kept bleach on for.

'Not very long on yours.'

Not very long! We'd been yacking away for ages. I screeched in anguish, slammed the phone down and ran for the bathroom.

Thursday 8.05 p.m.

So. I am now available to play on stage pretty much most characters from *Cats*, the musical. If you want to see what the whitest white and the orangiest orange look like, look no further than my noggin. With my usual darker blond hair striped in between.

What about school tomorrow? What about Chris Jones? Who wants to kiss a girl who looks like someone in a novelty wig?

I am in shock. I need hot sweet tea. Now.

Thursday 8.30 p.m.

I have been down to make some. I tied my hair up in a scarf. Luckily Ned wasn't around and Mum having a style bypass has advantages. She said, 'And what look is that, darling?'

'The look of someone whose life is officially over,' I thought but said nothing and came back here. I shall obviously have to stay at home until my hair grows out. Or get a small part at the back in the *The Lion King* show. How long does it take for hair to grow out? Six months? A year? I should have grabbed a packet of biscuits while I was down there. It is obvious that I cannot go to school until my hair is back to normal. Or to the party. It is not possible for Chris Jones to see me like this.

Thursday 8.45 p.m.

Mum has just knocked on the door with some toast and honey (this is so rare an event – I wonder if I am dying?). She thought I might like to know that she has just phoned Mrs Jones about the party. Mrs Jones will be in the house next door with Jennifer Cooper's parents and they will be keeping a close eye on the party. So I can go. Isn't that great news? She thought I'd be pleased.

I am fate's plaything.

★ RANI'S TIP ●

To bring out the <u>natural</u> highlights in fair hair, try this home treatment: Make a strong brew of camomile flowers (you can get them from the health shop or chemist). Put two big handfuls into a bowl of hot water (about one litre). When it has stewed for twenty minutes and the water is cool, strain it. Use this as a final rinse on washed hair.

For dark hair, use a large bunch of rosemary instead of camomile.

Chapter 12

Friday 7.30 a.m.

I am refusing to go to school. It is ludicrous to expect a girl to go out in public looking like this. Mum has obviously taken leave of her senses to even suggest it. I even came out, stood in front of my parents and pulled off my scarf to show them the full horror, but sometimes their hearts are stone. I have put the chair against the door but I don't think it will hold them back for much longer.

Friday 7.40 a.m.

It has gone quiet. I don't think this is a good thing. I have spoken to Chloe who suggested wearing the scarf for the party and going for a *Pirates of the Caribbean* look. Yeah right. Perhaps she might like to lend me an eye patch as well. And a hook. Rani just asked why I didn't wait until she could do it. Not really helpful at this stage.

Mum is knocking gently on the door. I see. It is Good Cop time. But I will not waver. NOTHING will make me go to school today.

Friday 8.15 a.m.

I am writing this on the bus. I cannot BELIEVE I am here. I have plaited my hair and pinned the plaits up to try and tuck as much of it away as I can. I look ridiculous. It was blackmail. Mum said she had spoken to Rani's mum and she had assured her she could sort out the problem if I went round to their place straight after school. She will put a toner on my hair to dye it back to as near as its original colour as she can. I would be able to go to the party. But only if I got dressed and out of my room 'right this minute'.

It is so, so cruel. Dr Jennings would be horrified by the insensitive nature of their parenting skills. I'm a whisker away from social services stepping in.

Rani has just asked me who Dr Jennings is.

'None of your business,' I have wittily replied.

Friday 8.25 a.m.

Rani was telling me that she thought that Dr Jennnings might want to talk to her for a deeper insight into my personality. And I was saying, 'No, she definitely wouldn't,' when Maddy and Sasha got on.

Maddy has begun her bragging about her wild times in America. The booze, the boys – we've heard about nothing else since she got the invite to the party. I can see that Sasha and Tess think it's all a laugh. It's not that Sasha is intentionally mean, it's that she doesn't have close friends like Rani and Chloe.

(Yes, Rani, very funny, get your head off my shoulder.)

Sasha is the cat that walks alone. She doesn't seem to need anyone. She doesn't take care or look out for anyone in particular. Least of all Maddy Velde.

Rani agrees. She is in a good mood because Mum has agreed to me going to the party. My mum not agreeing might have caused a difficult situation for her. Let us just hope she appreciates what it has cost me.

Rani says no one will notice my appearance.

Friday 8.35 a.m.

Doug Brennan just leaned over and asked, 'What's with the Tigger meets Heidi look?'

Nobody, but nobody, suffers as I do.

Friday 4.15 p.m.

On the bus now, recovering from a hideous day. Suffice to say, if anyone else begins to snigger and make little growling noises as I walk by, I will scream. Spent my time avoiding people. Naturally *today*, Chris Jones was round every corner. I had no option but to spend all my breaks in the loos. Chloe and Rani took it in turns to keep me company.

Yes, Rani – which *was* very kind. Oh really? My writing is hard to read? It's not my writing that's wobbly, it's the bus.

Then when I thought it was safe, I came out and undid a plait to peer into the mirror and see if the whiteness and orangeness had toned down at all (*no*), only to look up and see that Melanie and Jet had appeared and were holding each other up in the doorway.

It is incidents like that that keep people like Dr Jennings in employment.

Friday 7.00 p.m.

Things have got better since we got to Rani's house. I am deep conditioning my hair (bleach makes it like straw) and wearing a face mask at the moment. Rani will do my make-up later since she is doing Jennifer's now.

My Plan is whirring into action and after two long hours my hair is blissfully back to an approximation of its normal colour. Thank you, Mrs Ray.

I love Mrs Ray. She lets you use all her make-up which she keeps in a special room and try on her saris. Even though she isn't Indian like Rani's dad, she's got loads for special occasions. Rani's genius brother, Norman, is hiding in his room. He's Year Twelve and is frightened of girls in large numbers (i.e. more than one). He reminds me of a six-foot bushbaby with glasses. Rani despairs of him ever getting a girlfriend. I should help him out one day but at the moment I'm rather busy. I may need to start a waiting list. Chloe is showing me possible outfits for Jennifer.

Time to wash my hair and get this face mask off.

Friday 7.30 p.m.

Jennifer looks amazing. She is having a sandwich with Rani. I don't know how they can eat. (Well, I know how Rani can – nothing puts her off her food.)

Though I say it myself we have done a fabulous job. Jennifer's long hair has been blown dry and straightened. Rani changed her parting from the middle to the side so a sweep of hair is swinging across her face. Her pretty eyes are made up with grey-blue smudgy liner and mascara and her face looks glowing with a little foundation and a slick of pink gloss on her lips and cheeks.

She is wearing a green silk camisole of Chloe's and my short dark-blue gypsy skirt. Chloe has lent her a low-slung belt and her blue and green bead necklaces.

We had a problem with the shoes as she had only brought a pair of black court shoes. They were never going to do. Rani's feet were too small and mine were too big. Typically Chloe just sat down on the bed and pulled off her precious pale suede boots.

They were a high street copy of a Cerranti pair she'd seen in *Vogue*. She'd saved her pocket money for months to get them. Jennifer looked a bit dubious at first but Chloe said, 'Go on, I've got my trainers in my bag and I'm only going to be seeing my dad this weekend.'

She's that committed to getting a look right. I wished she was coming with us, but she wouldn't miss her weekends with her father for anything.

We have decided on my outfit too. Low-rise faded blue jeans with a white floaty top. It has tiny silver sequins around the neckline and on the sleeves. It's cropped short so you can see a bit of my stomach. Mum's lips would go in a straight line if she saw it, which only goes to show how great it is. Chloe has lent me some thin silver necklaces and a bracelet of small glass crystals and white stones. I am wearing some flat silver ballet-style pumps. Rani has done my make-up and got my hair all shiny and straight. If I say it myself I'm not looking bad at all. Rani is looking very cool in a black halter-neck and miniskirt. She has made a huge effort to make herself look older with lots of kohl round her huge hazel eyes and shiny plum lipstick and she has succeeded. If she can just get out of the house before her dad sees her . . . He is ultra-strict about what she wears and we don't want a repetition of the evening when he insisted she wear tracksuit bottoms under her miniskirt. Chloe has gone to get the bus to *her* dad's. She has made us promise to keep an eye out for Maddy.

We have promised.

What with Maddy, Jack, Jennifer and getting off with Chris Jones I have a lot on my plate this evening.

Rani's mum is shouting up the stairs. Time to go. When I next write in this diary I could have really and truly snogged Chris Jones.

CHLOE'S TIP ● ● ● ● ● ● ● ● ● ● ● ● ● ● ● ● ● ● ●

When dressing for a party, we all want to dazzle but it is important not to go too far and end up looking like a Christmas tree. Some tips: Parties are a great time for bold statements, but generally only one item of clothing that glitters per outfit is a good rule. Wear layers, because parties get really hot! You may love your fluffy mohair shrug, but after a couple of dance numbers, you'll be boiling. Always have something cool on underneath that you don't mind exposing.

Chapter 13

Friday 11.30 p.m.

It happened.

I have snogged the most experienced kisser in the school.

I have to admit it was much better than Danny. But owing to unforeseen circumstances I was prevented from giving this momentous experience my full concentration. It wasn't my fault. God knows.

Mrs Ray dropped us off and it was Jack who opened the door.

'Wow! You, you *all* look great. Come on in.'

But where was Chris?

We weren't the only ones looking good. Jack was making dark jeans and a cool T-shirt look very acceptable. I could see Jennifer was having to hold herself back from flinging her arms around him as he manoeuvred his way through the hall. As we passed the sitting room I saw what was keeping our host busy: Jet leaning against the wall, twirling her highlights and laughing like a hyena.

That was the first thing I was not prepared for.

A burst of loud laughter from the kitchen told me that Sasha's mates, the guys from the band, were here already. That would disappoint the boys from school. Although she's not going out with any of them as far as I know, no one was going to risk making a fool of themselves while they looked on.

Tess and Maddy were with them. Maddy was back in her old mask of black and white make-up and had back-combed her hair into a wild mess. I recognised the shirt and jumper from our first meeting. She must have no clothes at all. She was talking loudly and waving a cola bottle around, which by the state of her obviously didn't have just cola in it. One of the boys was Doug Brennan's brother, Wayne. He had his arm around her. As she took a huge swig from the bottle he was shouting encouragingly. Sasha was nowhere to be seen.

'I hope she knows what she's doing,' Rani muttered. 'We promised we'd keep an eye on her but if we go up to her, she'll only tell us to go away.'

Tom lumbered cheerfully up with Joe Carter, his giant footballing mate and all-round nice guy, and slapped Jack on the back. He put an arm over Rani's shoulder and an arm over mine. He raised his eyebrows at Jennifer.

'Looking great, Jenn.' He cast his eyes over Rani and me and sighed. 'Well, at least you tried.'

Rani thumped him over the head.

Jennifer blushed and said, 'How's your band, Jack?'

Good. Now we were getting somewhere.

He had a puzzled look and I jumped in, 'It's Jennifer, *remember*?'

And he said, 'Sure, yes, in the dining hall. You just look, er, sort of different tonight.'

Brilliant! I gave Rani a smug look, which she ignored.

'Really?' Jennifer was giggling now and running her fingers through her hair. 'I've heard your music. I think it's so great that you write your own songs. It must be so hard to think of things to write about.'

Good again. Everyone knows that it's important to show interest in what people do.

'Er, no,' said Jack. 'Not really difficult. I enjoy it.'

'What gives you your inspiration?' If Jennifer's lashes had batted much faster she'd have taken off.

'Inspiration? I don't know, everything really, emotions, people, love, life, that kind of stuff.'

'Love! Ooh, have you ever written a song about a girl you know?'

'Er . . .' Jack's turn to blush now. 'Thought about it but not put it down on paper yet.'

'Why not?'

'I don't know what the ending is yet.'

For a confusing moment he seemed to be looking straight at me, but a deafening barrage of shouting behind my back made me see what had really attracted his attention. Wayne was banging on the fridge door chanting while Maddy was taking yet another slug.

Tom frowned.

Joe asked, 'Is she OK? She's going to be seriously ill if she carries on like that.'

'She's trying to impress Sasha,' I replied. 'But she's gone into the next room and left Maddy to fend for herself.'

Jack said maybe he should go over but Jennifer squeaked 'NO!' so loudly that we all jumped.

She flushed. 'It's just that, it's just that, er, she'll only say something rude to look big in front of the others.'

Joe, who had looked like he was going to go over with Jack, shrugged his shoulders and wandered off frowning.

Tom changed the subject, saying, 'Come on then, ladies, who wants a dance? Remember I am spoken for so keep your hands to yourselves, but you'll get to see my new groovy dance moves.'

You really *don't* want to see any of Tom's dance moves. It's a wonder Chloe is still in one piece. He started flinging himself about 'to warm up'.

Then Jet's familiar foghorn laugh erupted from the next room and went straight through me. I was beginning to wonder if I'd made a huge mistake. Had I read the signals so wrong? Had the macaroni, the mud and tiger-hair proved obstacles too hard to overcome? I was beginning to wish that I hadn't blabbed about the Chris thing so much.

I should have played it down.

But I *never* can do that. I've always longed to be the mysterious girl who says very little and everyone finds intriguing. If you have this quality you don't have to be funny or make an effort or anything. And boys still think you're wonderful.

It's a cat-like quality. Sasha has it. You never quite know what she feels about things, which makes you want to know what she feels about things. But I'm not like that. I am a dog person who runs around with a waggy tail sharing every detail of my life. And now look where it's got me. Humiliation. And the worst bit is I know it won't be the last time.

I am doomed to spend the rest of my life failing to be a cat-person.

I was feeling a bit tragic about all of this when I looked up to see Jack saying, 'Carrie?' and holding out his hand. I was mortified. He'd seen my face fall and now he felt sorry for me. In front of everyone as well. Who all seemed to be staring at me.

Jennifer was giving me a look.

And it was not a friendly look.

This was a disaster. I thought quickly and saved the situation by shrugging my shoulders and saying, 'I'm not really in the mood at the moment, don't like this song much.'

Then there was another loud laugh, Chris's this time. Jack didn't move but stood there, looking at me intently. No doubt thinking he was being made a total fool of.

I needed to rescue the situation. I gave Jennifer a nudge in his direction and said, 'I'm sure Jennifer would like a dance though.'

Jennifer's head started to do the nodding-dog-in-car impersonation (not a cat-person *at all*) and she grabbed his arm and propelled him firmly in the direction of the dance floor.

'She's not that shy after all, is she?' Rani said, staring after her.

'I know,' I said proudly. 'Our makeover has done wonders for her confidence, hasn't it?'

'So it seems. But, Carrie, I just want to remind you that I still don't think your ultimate plan is going to succeed. In fact, let me see, who were those people who thought that the Jack-Jennifer thing was a good idea? Oh yes, I remember now. *You.*'

'Why so negative, Rani? Look!' And I pointed out that they had gone off to dance together.

'Jack had no choice! You *made* him dance with her. He wanted to dance with YOU!'

Yes, I thought, but only because he felt sorry for me. Then Tom came dancing back in as he'd just realised he was dancing on his own and Rani went off. She was going to have a look around the dance floor and see if anyone caught her eye. I had already seen Kenny Lee looking longingly at her. He's in Year Eleven. And he's cute. Not very tall but that's not an issue for Rani. He's got black spiky hair, blue eyes and a cheeky grin. I know she likes him but she says she's so worried about her desperation showing through that she feels it's best to keep cool.

I was going next door to go up to Chris and say hello, but then I heard them laugh again and I lost my nerve.

I didn't want to see Jet flirting with Chris thank you very much. A girl has her pride. Had my mum phoning his mum put him off me forever?

So I stood there with that horrible feeling that everyone is staring at you and thinking that you have no friends.

I wanted to write a placard and put it round my neck and it would say this:

> *I HAVE LOADS OF FRIENDS AND A FULL SOCIAL LIFE.*
> *SO DO NOT PITY ME.*
> *I AM TEMPORARILY CHOOSING TO ENJOY MY*
> *OWN COMPANY IN A RELAXED AND TOTALLY*
> *UNCONCERNED WAY, OK?*

I thought that just about covered it. And I took a huge handful of cheese and onion crisps out of the bowl on the table and stuffed them into my mouth. I was thinking that the placard idea was a winner. You could have one for when you trip over in the street or your skirt gets caught in your knickers:

> *PLEASE DO NOT THINK FOR ONE MINUTE THAT*
> *I AM FEELING FOOLISH.*
> *I AM SO OVER IT ALREADY.*
> *IN FACT I HAVE ALREADY COMPLETELY FORGOTTEN*
> *WHAT I DID, I AM SO OVER IT.*

Mmmm. That one might need fine-tuning.

I took another handful of crisps.

'Carrie! Babe!'

I wished I had another placard now.

It would say:

COULD YOU GO AWAY AND COME BACK
IN ONE MINUTE EXACTLY?

I did the best smile I could while chomping on a ton of cheese and onion crisps. So unattractive. Unlike Chris who was looking gorgeous in faded denims and pale blue shirt. His blond hair flopped over his blue-green eyes. I resisted my desire to collapse against his manly form with relief and gratitude.

'I've been looking everywhere for you.'

Not that hard you haven't, I thought. But my heart was so flooded with my escape from social disgrace that I pushed that negative vibe away.

So AT LAST I was on the dance floor with my true love. Even though I was desperately poking my tongue around my mouth to try and excavate the last traces of crisps and wondering if there was any toothpaste in the house.

But back on track for some serious snogging.

Friday 11.55 p.m.

Mum just came in (pink furry slippers, red pyjama bottoms and one of Dad's T-shirts) and told me if I don't go to sleep right away I will be too tired to be of any help at Chloe's house tomorrow. I am now writing under the covers by torchlight.

Where was I? Right, dancing away, feeling brilliant.

And then the second thing I hadn't prepared for happened.

I could see Kenny dancing with Rani and gave her the thumbs up. I knew she would kill me later but I couldn't resist it. I was thinking everyone is having such a great time, everyone except that girl all alone on the sofa. Now who is that?

Jennifer! Jennifer all alone on the sofa and looking very much in need of my *I HAVE LOADS OF FRIENDS*, etc. placard. Where had Jack gone? Calm down, I thought. Do not get hysterical, he's probably just gone to get a drink or perhaps he's, he's ... DANCING WITH SASHA DOOLEY!

Chris was looking at me strangely now so I took some deep breaths and closed my eyes. But when I opened them again Sasha was still slinking around Jack with her sexy cat-person moves. It took all my self-control not to go over and haul her out of there by the collar of her tiny black silk jacket.

You cannot leave people on their own for ten minutes. Do I have to be everywhere?

Now I had to add Jennifer's forlorn figure to my list of responsibilities. She was looking at me mournfully as if I should do something. Then Jack stopped dancing and said something to Sasha. Too close, Buster! Get you mouth away from her ear. Jennifer wilted further into the sofa and Jack headed for the kitchen.

So I told Chris I'd be back in a moment and followed him.

I tapped Jack sharply on the back and he turned round, surprised.

'Can I help you?' he asked.

'What's going on?' I demanded.

'Excuse me?' He looked bewildered.

'What's going on with Sasha Dooley?'

'Well, let me see. I thought it was called *having a dance*. You know, it's when you move your body in time to the music. People do it at parties. You make some moves like this . . .'

Short demonstration.

'And if you are someone like Chris Jones you mouth the lyrics and scrunch up you face as if in pain. Like this . . .'

'Ha ha, very funny. You *know* what I mean.'

'No, what *do* you mean, Carrie?'

'I mean . . . I mean . . .'

What did I mean?

'I mean what about Jennifer?'

'What about her?'

'You asked her to dance and then you just *dumped* her! For Sasha Dooley. Can't you see how upset she is?'

And he said, 'Whoa! Hold on a minute. I did *not* ask her to dance. I actually asked *you* to dance, if you remember. You said no and then put me into a position where I *had* to dance with her.'

This made me feel uncomfortable so I chose to ignore it. 'Jennifer's so lovely. What's wrong with her?'

'Nothing's wrong with her. She said she wanted to sit down, Sasha came over and asked me to dance and that was that.'

That was that! I don't *think* so. What about poor Jennifer?

And then I got annoyed and told him that if he'd had half a brain he would have known that Jennifer had wanted him to go and sit down next to her.

Then he got annoyed and said, 'Did I miss something, because I didn't realise I had to apply to Carrie, Chief of the Party Police for written permission to get on the dance floor.'

I snapped. 'There's a girl on the sofa next door with a broken heart because of you.'

He snapped back. 'No, because of you! And I'll tell you something else. I vote *you* the worst judge I know of who I like and don't like.'

Well! I was outraged. Everyone knows I'm sensitive and very emotionally intelligent.

My hands went on my hips at this point, which is never a good sign, and I'd just managed to say, 'Oh really? And do you know something? You are making the biggest mistake . . .'

And then the third unexpected (and unwelcome) thing happened.

12.35 a.m.

Dad just came in and said that Mum said I will never be allowed to go to another party ever again unless I get some sleep NOW! They do not understand that it is crucial that Dr Jennings gets things hot off the press, full of raw emotion as it were, but I would like to be able to leave my house again so I'll have to finish in the morning. And I haven't even got to the snogging bit yet.

 **CARRIE'S TIP** •

When decorating a room for parties, concentrate on walls and overhead where your efforts can be appreciated by a crowded room of people. Good old fairy lights are useful again here. Old CDs stuck on the ceiling and walls, or hanging like mobiles look good – or you can just cut out big foil circles. An old sheet, dyed and draped over furniture, not only protects it but also can hide less than lovely fabric.

Chapter 14

Saturday 9.00 a.m.

I have just returned from seeing myself in the bathroom mirror.
Yuck. I will give my hair a wash and put on a lick of mascara later.
I need to finish my faithful recording of the events of last night
before I go round to Chloe's flat to work on her surprise room
makeover.

There was a third thing that happened. As I was with Jack, doing
my hands-on-hips-fishwife impression in the kitchen, a cry of
'Timber!' went up by the fridge. Maddy's legs had buckled. She
was being propped up by Wayne and Tess. Even with all that
make-up on you could see she was green.

'I think I'm going to be sick,' she mumbled and they sprang
away. Jack and I leaped forward to catch her. I put her arm over
my shoulder and then Rani appeared and I said could she help.
Sensing it was a girls only moment, I said, 'Take the other arm
from Jack.' I could see Sasha wandering in looking for him with
Jennifer not far behind.

'No, I can help,' he said.

I jerked my head towards the door and said primly, 'I think
you're too busy. We'll be fine.'

He opened his mouth as if he was going to say something and
then Maddy began to moan.

Rani took the other arm, saying, 'Come on, we've got to get
her to the bathroom, quick!'

Jack hesitated and then stood aside.

We hoisted her through the hall and up the stairs (not easy). Jennifer followed us up. 'What happened, Carrie? You said I'd have more confidence if I had the make-over, and that boys would notice me but Jack *still* doesn't seem interested.'

Maddy was moaning again.

'Can we talk about this another time, Jennifer? I'm a bit busy at the moment,' I grunted. She gave me a long hard glare, then flounced back down the stairs.

Rani raised her eyebrows. 'What have we done? We've created a monster!'

'Don't be silly,' I snapped, as I heard Jennifer stomp downstairs.

I was aware that I had left Chris Jones down there in the clutches of Jet again. And Jack with Sasha.

Rani peered up at me from under Maddy's armpit.

'What's up with you?'

'Jack Harper is making the biggest mistake of his life.'

'Wow,' said Rani with a grin. 'The biggest mistake *of his life*. That's a pretty big mistake.'

We shouldered open the bathroom door and had just got Maddy through and shut it behind us when there was a sharp tap, tap. We shuffled Maddy around to open it again.

It was Jennifer.

'Carrie, I really need to talk to you. They're sitting on the sofa and she's all snuggled up to him, whispering in his ear.'

I ground my teeth. That's what *I* was supposed to be doing (but with Chris, obviously).

Maddy was starting to heave, but Jennifer kept asking what to do and wouldn't go. And then the last unexpected and most horrible thing happened. Maddy threw up all over Chloe's pale suede boots. Jennifer looked down, squealed in horror and ran out.

Rani looked at me and sighed. 'Isn't this just turning out to be the best evening ever?'

She held Maddy's head over the toilet bowl and I unrolled metres of loo roll and surveyed the damage. I pinched a squeeze of toothpaste before I began cleaning up. I am ever the multi-tasking optimist.

I knew I might be blowing my last chance with Chris. But I had promised myself I would put Friends First, and my help was needed. And if you want to be a better person, you take care of people. It can be very inconvenient at times but you have to do it. I felt sure Rani wished she was downstairs playing hard to get with Kenny but she wasn't complaining.

Maddy hauled herself to her feet and washed her face. Her make-up had smudged and streaked. She looked at her reflection in the mirror. Her face crumpled. Then she took a deep breath. She screwed her face up in a sneer.

'You can go,' she said coldly. 'I can look after myself.'

Neither Rani nor I moved.

'I just think, perhaps . . .' Rani murmured.

'JUST GO!' Maddy shouted. She put her hands on the basin to steady herself.

'Maddy . . .' I ventured gingerly. She looked so vulnerable standing there, in spite of trying to seem so tough and in control. 'We just want to help . . .'

Then I saw a large tear plop into the sink, quickly followed by another. Rani saw it too.

'Honestly, you don't have to stay,' Maddy croaked, but more

gently. 'My mum is picking me up any minute.' Poor girl, she really was feeling terrible.

I quietly turned on the cold tap and wet a flannel. I passed it to her and she covered her face with it.

'F-franx,' Maddy whispered through the flannel.

Rani's head went up and her eyes opened wide.

'What was that?'

Maddy lowered the cloth slowly. 'Thank you,' she said.

'That's OK.' I smiled at her and she had just managed a small wobbly smile in return when suddenly her face fell.

'Oh my God, did I just throw up over someone's boots?'

Rani and I looked at each other but said nothing.

'I did. I threw up over Jennifer's boots. Oh no.' She put her head in her hands.

'They weren't Jennifer's,' Rani chipped in. 'They were Chloe's.'

Maddy looked horrified. She swore she'd make it up to Chloe and pay her back in some way. I could see why she was so upset. She obviously had no money so I don't see how she could.

She began wringing the flannel in her hands. 'God, why can't I get anything right.' She looked directly at us. 'I'm so sorry; you must think I'm such a joke. And I thought I was doing so well this evening. Not so impressive now.' She gave a low moan. 'Oh no, what will they think of me?'

'You don't want to worry about what they think, Maddy,' I said firmly. 'Sasha hangs out with some strange people. She's a pretty "live for the moment" kind of girl. She doesn't depend on them for anything and they know not to depend on her.'

'You depend on each other though, don't you? You and Chloe and Rani.'

There was a pause.

'You know we have *tried* to be friendly,' I murmured. 'I know the woods incident was . . . um, a bit weird, but I did have your best interests at heart.'

'I know you did. I got you girls wrong. I thought you were pretending to be friendly so you could then laugh at me or . . . or for the wrong reasons. I know now it wasn't you who was laughing at me on the bus the first day of term as well.'

'I was a bit of an idiot when we met at Barnaby's, you know, when my mum was going to ask . . .'

'Forget it, I don't blame you. I had been seriously rude to you both. But I could see straight away that you were the type of pretty, confident girls who everyone likes. The type of girl who would think I was just a freak. I was so convinced that you were going to hate me anyway, I thought I'd just speed up the process. And I'm also sorry that you fell over on the field when you were chasing me out of the wood.'

The massive humiliation came flooding back to me.

'Oh,' said Rani to Maddy, seeing my face colour, 'and you were doing *so* well up till then.'

But it had reminded me that Chris Jones was downstairs without me and the music had got smoochy. Which was when Jennifer's head came round the door again.

'Carrie – serious emergency. It's slow dancing.'

'I'll be down in a minute, Jennifer,' I said.

Jennifer pouted. 'I don't think we've got that long,' she said and disappeared, slamming the door behind her.

Rani clapped her hands together. 'It's all going so marvellously well, isn't it, Carrie?'

Maddy looked puzzled. 'What is?'

Rani put her arm around Maddy's shoulder. 'Never mind,' she said. 'It's a long story.'

Maddy winced. 'I hope I didn't mess anything up for you two this evening.'

'Er, nothing serious.'

'It's just that I know I've behaved like a complete jerk, but actually, I really . . . well, think you're both pretty cool and you've been so kind to me this evening. I know the person I've been since I got here isn't the kind of person you'd want to hang around with, but . . .'

Rani gave me an encouraging nudge with her spare elbow.

'Maddy, what are you doing tomorrow?' I asked.

'What? Well, nothing . . .'

'Great. What I mean is, we're planning a surprise for Chloe and we need as much help as we can get. Is there any chance you could get round to her house tomorrow morning? It would be brilliant if you could. It would really help us out.'

Maddy went bright red and nodded. So we gave her the address. If she's not feeling too ill, we hope she'll be coming later today.

Jennifer reappeared at the door. You could see now that though some effort had been made to clean up the boots they were never going to be the same again.

'Maddy's mum is here to collect her,' she said, glaring at me.

'Jennifer you look fantastic, what did you do?' Maddy blurted out.

'Carrie, Rani and Chloe helped me. Carrie said it would make someone notice me. But you were wrong about that weren't you, Carrie?'

Rani gave me a 'I told you so' look. So I said desperately, 'Honestly, Jennifer, don't get upset about it. There are plenty of other great boys around. Jack's not that much of a catch anyway. He's way too intense and some people don't think he's that good looking.' (Blind people possibly.)

Jennifer looked at me like I felt – as if I was very, very stupid. Then she turned on the ruined boots and left.

And to Rani's credit she didn't go on about it (that much). She just said, 'Hadn't you better be getting downstairs and be getting that snog?'

'What about you? You were pretty keen too,' I replied.

'I don't think I want my first proper snog to be a rushed thing at the end of such a mad evening like this. I'll keep with my treat 'em mean, keep 'em keen approach. Your snog, on the other hand, is a predestined snog so you'd better get moving.'

So I did.

Chris was coming out of the kitchen when I went downstairs. He gave me a huge smile. 'There you are! Been tending the sick I hear. She's just leaving. She's a bit of a loser, isn't she? I mean, if they measured beauty in pounds she'd be Miss World, though.'

'That's a mean thing to say!' I snapped. Chris looked astonished and started apologising and asking me to dance and launching into a Mr Love Pants Charm Offensive.

After what he'd said I didn't really feel like dancing, but then I saw Sasha and Jack dancing together so I took a deep breath and said, 'OK'.

So we danced and he pulled me closer and I thought that just a few hours earlier this would have seemed like the most wonderful thing in the world. But now I couldn't stop thinking about how Jack and Sasha had ruined Jennifer's evening (but really knowing it was me). How was I to know that Sasha Dooley might be interested in Jack? She never goes out with boys in school. And how was I to know that he liked her? He had been right. I hadn't the faintest clue what was going on in his head. Anyway, *The Snog At Last*.

As I was leaning on Chris's shoulder I caught Jack's eye across the room. I gave him a cold glare and nestled closer into Chris. Jack then gave me a defiant look and started to stroke Sasha's hair (what she has of it – it's very short compared to mine) and she moved her face in front of his so he absolutely had no choice *at all* but to kiss her. She was practically forcing him. Absolutely outrageous behaviour. Typical of Sasha – she doesn't care what she does. And then Chris was saying something in my ear about how lovely I was and then he kissed me with all his years of kissing experience. And all I could think about was that I hoped Jack was watching to see how much I didn't care about the fact he was making such a huge mistake with Sasha. The really maddening thing was although I was with the world's best kisser, the thrill of the moment was totally ruined.

So there it is.

Like I said. I can only look forward to the next time, when my mind will be free from really annoying distractions and I can get the full benefit.

Saturday 9.30 a.m.

Mum is now banging on the door saying if I want any breakfast I have to come down, NOW!

And now I must gather my energies for curtain-making and

painting and suchlike. Actually I am very excited about it all. Except seeing Jack. Because he is coming with Tom today. Which I am nervous about because I suspect he is still going to be mad at me for interfering at the party. Maybe I shouldn't have said anything to him. But everyone knows that Sasha never gets serious about anyone and I just think he's the sort of boy who is looking for someone really special to have a relationship with. Mind you, now Jennifer has turned from shy and retiring into a rampaging Diva, I'm not so sure she's the one either.

Plus there's the joy of meeting up with my spider pal again. Rani says we have to catch it before we start. In case it gets hurt.

★ 🕶 RANI'S TIP •
To revive a tired face after a late night: blend half a cucumber and one small pot of plain yogurt. Dab this over a cleansed face. Next place a cold, used teabag over each eye. Then lie back and relax for ten minutes. Rinse face with cold water before moisturising.

Chapter 15

It is almost impossible to be this dirty. But it has all been worth it. Chloe's room is going to be *sooo* beautiful.

Mum drove Rani and me over to Chloe's house this morning so that we could take the chest of drawers, a little desk and an old rug from Max's room. Rani's mum had also donated a small wooden chair and showed us two saris we could have for decoration. One was white with tiny silver stars and the other was a deep pink silk. We decided we'd leave them with her as we would be doing the sewing there. I was in heaven imagining curtains and cushions, while Rani's dad piled pots of white paint into the car.

Rani sat clutching an empty plastic box with holes in it on her lap. On top of it balanced a notebook with the list of things we had to do today. For a mad person she is very well organised.

Mrs Simmonds offered us croissants and hot chocolate when we arrived. (Jim was at a friend's house since keeping secrets is not one of his strengths.) Rani said no thanks but we'd love them later. Then she firmly tapped her notepad with her pen and began prodding me in the back with it all the way up the stairs. Did I say organised? Some people might say bossy.

First thing to do on list: *Catch spider.*

The next fifteen minutes involved a lot of me wandering around vaguely scanning the floor saying, 'It's not here is it?' in a hopeful tone. Then, with the swiftness of a creature that has recently done SAS training, the spider threw itself off a beam and parachuted *on to my hair*. I screamed. There was a scuffle, Rani yelling, 'Don't hurt it, don't hurt it!' and finally the successful capture – from *off my head*. I shall be needing extra time in therapy now.

Rani then got out her notebook, made a tick and went downstairs to put the plastic box away safely. Apparently the spider was going to have a new home in her dad's shed.

She came back up and I could hear someone following her. I tensed up because I thought it might be Jack. I wasn't sure how he was going to be feeling about seeing me this morning. I even wondered if he'd still come. But it was Maddy. Looking like death. In old jeans and T-shirt with her hair scraped back. She didn't need make-up to have a white face this morning. She managed a weak smile.

'Are you sure you feel up to this?' I asked.

'It's the least I can do after last night. If I can do anything to help I will. I feel so terrible about those boots.'

I don't blame her. I knew Chloe would understand but it would be a tremendous blow. Because Maddy didn't have a lot of clothes and things, I think she understood how bad Chloe might feel.

Rani was tapping her notebook again and looking meaningfully at her watch.

Next thing to do on list: *Take up carpet*.

So we began. We ripped back the rotting carpet, to expose the wooden floorboards underneath. Chloe's mum had checked already in a corner to see that they were in good condition.

Coughing and wheezing, we shoved the shreds into bin-liners and lugged them downstairs. Then we swept and vacuumed.

Third thing to do on the list: *Clean the walls, floor and windows.*

We filled buckets with lots of hot soapy water. We scrubbed. We mopped. We wiped.

It was satisfying to see the thick dirt disappearing and the original colour of wood and paint start to come through.

'So what happened after I left the party?' asked Maddy, breaking through the noise of sloshing water and scrubbing.

'Carrie got off with Mr Love Pants,' Rani replied.

Maddy looked puzzled then pleased. 'Well, hey! That's just great. I'm so relieved looking after me didn't blow it for you.' He is a cute-looking guy. You were pretty popular last night, weren't you?'

I didn't know what she meant so I didn't say anything.

She continued, 'You know when Jennifer and I went downstairs Jack was searching for you. Since Chris had been, er, talking to Jet and Sasha was throwing out the guys from the band, I guess that Jack thought he might have a chance after all . . .' She put her head in her hands and groaned. 'Will I ever live that night down?'

Although I was very sympathetic to Maddy's pain I felt compelled not to let her get distracted from the important part of the story. The part with me in it. 'I think you must have got that wrong, Maddy. Jack isn't the slightest bit interested in me like that.' In fact I'm sure he thinks I'm an interfering control freak.

'Really?' Maddy said. 'If you say so, but when he asked us where you were, Jennifer said the weirdest thing.'

But I didn't get to hear what the weirdest thing was because my mobile rang and it was Chris! (Swoon!) He wanted to know if I could see him this afternoon. He was missing me! I said no not today, and he said what about tomorrow and I had to say tomorrow wouldn't work either. Chloe's room was definitely a two-day job. And it was Friends First for me. I was not falling back in the Danny trap. I suggested he came over and helped out but he wasn't very keen.

'Next week then,' he said. 'See you.'

He didn't sound pleased. Rani, who had been listening closely to my conversation, gave me one of her knowing looks. It made me feel defensive so I started scrubbing furiously in the depths of the cupboard and said loudly, 'I know what you are thinking but he's dreamy, dreamy gorgeous and a fantastically experienced kisser.'

Silence.

I turned around slowly. Jack was standing in the doorway. I couldn't read his expression.

Brilliant.

Tom saved the situation by barging in, sloshing two buckets of water, and saying, 'More clean water for the ladies. We're off downstairs to paint furniture.' Which was a relief because to say Jack had not given me a warm greeting would be an understatement. An unsmiling 'Hi' and he left the room.

When you like and respect people it's not a good feeling when you know they don't feel the same way about you.

I threw myself into my work while Rani took the opportunity to ask Maddy lots of questions about her school in Los Angeles.

'I hated it,' she said. 'I would try to fit in and pretend to like the things the popular kids did, but they always know when you're different. Like you're faking it. I wonder what it must be like not even having to think about fitting in. It all just coming naturally . . .'

'People who aren't part of the crowd in school can be excellent independent thinkers, you know,' Rani said.

Wow. Move over Dr Jennings.

'Lots of successful, creative people found school tough. It was obviously difficult in America but you may have learned more than you realise from the experience. Nearly everyone feels left out sometimes,' Rani continued. 'Even Carrie has moments of self-doubt.'

I flicked my scrubbing brush at her.

'Everyone has their strengths, too. You must have something you like doing, you know, that you enjoy?'

Maddy went quiet and then said, 'I love taking pictures.'

It turned out she was mad about it.

'Have you got your camera here?' I asked. She had and took some photos of the room and Rani and me, 'To remind us what it was like before we change it all.'

'Perhaps we should take some of you,' Rani suggested.

'You mean to remind me of what I was like when you first saw me?'

'Aren't you going to look like that again?' I asked.

'No. That started because I couldn't look the same as everyone else so I thought I'd be as different as I could.'

'It *was* an interesting look,' Rani said hesitantly.

Maddy looked anxious, 'Do you think I look too boring now?'

'No!' We chorused.

'I know I'm fat and everything. I've tried every diet that's going but I can't stick to them.'

'It's got to be exercise,' Rani said firmly. 'Diets make you obsessed with food. You could start jogging.'

I thought Rani might have gone too far here, but Maddy said she would but she was too embarrassed to run outside.

'For goodness' sake,' Rani spluttered, 'you're not *that* big. We'll help you out. We'll take it in turns to run with you.'

Would we? Apart from our short amble around the playing field, the furthest any of us had run lately was for the bus. What with the cleaning and everything, being a better person was turning out to be more physically tiring than expected.

Much, much later, after Rani had crossed off the last item on the list for the day, Tom and Jack brought the painted furniture upstairs (looking very pretty) and put it on some newspaper. The fireplace has been scoured clean now and pretty, decorated tiles have emerged from the grimy surround. Opposite it, the once murky window panes sparkle in bleached and sanded wooden frames. Above, in the tent-shaped roof, the beams are no longer festooned with cobwebs, and on the floor the pale, scrubbed boards look fresh and ready for painting.

I was pleased to see how impressed the boys were with our hard work, even though Jack avoided speaking to me personally. I wanted to apologise to him for getting mad about the Jennifer thing. (I still feel Sasha's totally wrong for him – though I won't be saying that – *obviously*). I'll try to find an opportunity tomorrow.

Which reminds me, what *was* the weird thing that Jennifer said to him? She never told me. I will ask Maddy in the morning.

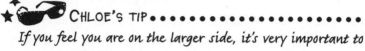 CHLOE'S TIP ● ● ● ● ● ● ● ● ● ● ● ● ● ● ● ● ● ● ●

If you feel you are on the larger side, it's very important to wear well-fitting clothes. Swamping yourself in huge, baggy clothes makes you look huge and baggy and squeezing into outfits that are too tight will make you look bigger, not smaller. Go for the best quality and fit you can.

Chapter 16

Sunday 7.00 p.m.

Well, I wish I hadn't asked. I am cringing as I write.

Maddy said that Jack had asked where I was. Jennifer's face had gone peculiar and she had said to him, 'Look, I realise that you think you're pretty popular this evening but you are *totally* wasting your time with Carrie. She's only interested in Chris Jones. And she has just told me that she thinks you are way too intense and she doesn't find you at all attractive. I'm only telling you this so you don't make A COMPLETE FOOL OUT OF YOURSELF. I know how painful *that* can be.'

And then she stomped out of the house.

I know that she had had a stressful and disappointing evening but I wish, I wish she hadn't said that. It wasn't even *true*. I only said those things to make her feel better. It didn't occur to me that she would repeat them to Jack. So now he thinks I'm a bossy, interfering girl who also thinks he's weird and ugly. No wonder he was so unfriendly yesterday. And today was worse.

I managed to get him alone in the kitchen in a break from painting, which wasn't easy as he was obviously avoiding me. Rani said I'd be a good stalker.

'Look, Jack,' I said. 'I want to apologise for Friday night. I had no right to be angry with you. The Jennifer thing was my fault, no one else's. I'm so sorry.'

He shrugged his shoulders and said, 'That's OK. It all seemed to work out by the end, didn't it?' He gave me a level look.

Duh, no!

For *me* maybe, but not for him, getting off with Sasha Dooley who eats boys for breakfast. And has quite short hair.

But I felt at least he was talking to me, so I ventured, 'Maddy told me what Jennifer said to you when they came downstairs.'

And that was my big mistake.

His dark eyes flashed. 'Did she? Yeah, well, it was a confusing evening, easy to mis-read situations. Although Jennifer obviously hadn't misunderstood what you said to her. So let's just leave each other's lives alone from now on, shall we?'

And before I could say anything else he turned and walked out.

Bugger.

The rest of the day was simply hard work. In spite of the awkwardness with Jack it *was* fantastic to see the room transformed by the white paint. The floor was sanded now. Tom and Jack agreed to come and varnish the floorboards after school when Chloe took Jim swimming. Thank goodness this room was up the little staircase and too far away for her to smell the fresh paint. It looked light and bright and the sun streamed through the sparkling window. Maddy wanted to take pictures. She said she was so aware that all around us these tiny interactions were taking place. A camera could catch them before they were gone forever. She felt she might miss something without it. However, as the mess was going to be so serious today, she had reluctantly left it behind.

I was glad she didn't have her camera out to catch the tiny interactions going on between Jack and me. He'd only looked in my direction once since our little chat and I think I could faithfully describe his expression as cool. In the ice and snow sense. I thought about trying to explain again but couldn't find the right moment.

I feel lousy about it. Also, I ache all over. My body is not used to manual labour. I am going to run a bath and have a scented soak in some of Mum's expensive oils.

Sunday 8.00 p.m.

I am wrapped in Mum's big soft towelling robe (a birthday present from Dad) and feeling physically, if not emotionally, restored.

Rani has just phoned to make sure we have all got our stories right about the weekend in case Chloe asks. We will not give away the secret, even under torture.

Chloe doesn't even know about our breakthrough with Maddy yet.

Or about her boots. We'll have to fill her in tomorrow – she's going to a gallery opening with her dad and won't be back until seriously late.

I am heading downstairs to find some chocolate. Mum went to the supermarket today and I know where she keeps her stash.

Sunday 8.20 p.m.

Mum has stripped me of my lovely towelling robe, but she let me keep the chocolate. She said I'd worked hard all weekend and deserved a treat. I've just eaten the whole huge bar but it doesn't matter, as I will be running it off this week thanks to Rani 'Road Runner' Ray. Rani is starting the running tomorrow. She's going to get the early bus to Pitsford and run to school with Maddy.

Maddy asked to meet her in the lane, up where the big houses are. I feel sad she doesn't want us to know where she lives. The idea is they will shower in the changing rooms before registration. Hmmm.

Glad it's not me. I must rest my weary bones.

Zzzzzz.

Sunday 10.30 p.m.

Was woken up by my mobile ringing. It was Chris! He wants to know if he can see me tomorrow after school.

Yes. Yes. Yes.

'Great,' he said. 'Meet me at my place at eight-thirty. My parents are going out for the evening.'

Eight-thirty! On a Monday night! His house!

I will need to think how to get round this with Mum. Even with not mentioning the lack of parents it's going to be a tough one.

I'm sure I can convince her how important it is to me, though. She will not want to stand between me and true happiness.

 CARRIE'S TIP •

White and cream instantly brighten up a room. Cheap white or cream thin cotton bedspreads, thrown over your bed or draped over chairs and tables, can give a room a real lift and make it look more coordinated.

Chapter 17

Monday 7.30 a.m.

Mum has ruined my life and I will never speak to her again.

I gave her twenty minutes of carefully constructed argument over breakfast, which she listened to carefully with a lot of 'Yes, I see' and head nodding. I finished with the lines, 'And that's why it's so important that I go. I know you will understand.'

Mum lifted her head up to look at me, smiled breezily and simply said, 'Never going to happen, Carrie.'

Which didn't give me a lot to play with. So I said it all again but with more urgency.

Then I said it pleading.

Then I said it wailing.

Then I stormed out of the kitchen, slammed the door and came back up here.

I am beside myself with frustration at Mum's lack of under-standing. I could tear my red acrylic jumper asunder. She will never know the damage that she has done to me. First insisting on phoning Chris's mum about the party and now this.

All I want is a bit of smooth tarmac on the road of life, but fate and Mum keep making potholes in it.

That is very deep. I will keep that for Dr Jennings. At least she will understand. But what about Chris Jones?

Monday 6.15 p.m.

No Rani or Maddy on the bus this morning. Due to the running.

Felt lonely. Also felt mad and anxious about having to tell Chris I couldn't go round this evening. Sasha Dooley stopped as she swayed past and gave me a big grin.

'Great night on Friday, wasn't it?'

I managed to crank up a smile.

'Looking forward to today?' she gave me a knowing look.

No! I thought, but gave her a tight smile. Thanks to her I've got a very difficult conversation ahead of me with Jennifer Cooper. And Jack Harper hates me. Fake smiling was making my cheeks hurt.

'See you then,' she said in her oh-so-casual way and she made her way along the bus to Tess. No doubt to answer questions about her conquest on Friday night. I bet her mum lets her stay up all hours.

I cheered myself up by thinking about *my* conquest on Friday night. At least I hadn't had to sexually assault my dance partner to get a snog. And Chris *had* asked me on a date. Twice now. Even though, thanks to my mother/jailer, I couldn't go on it. I was going to have to suggest The Coffee Bean for a drink after school instead and he would think I was sadder than sad. It's pretty quiet in the week, so at least it would be just the two of us and I would get another chance with him without any annoying distractions.

Chloe met me off the bus. I told her about the boots straight away but she already knew. Jennifer had dropped them off at her place the night before. She'd also seen Maddy arriving at school from her run with Rani. Chloe said that Maddy had been so apologetic that she couldn't be angry. It's not as if she'd done it on purpose and maybe she could clean them up. That is the kind person she is. Other people might have ranted and raved and borne grudges. Not her. She is so worth the hours I spent last night getting white paint out of my hair. Even if it still has a faint whiff of turpentine.

I told her about the rest of the party and the unreasonableness of my mother on the way inside. She was sympathetic about this, but not as shocked at the failure of my plan with Jack as I had anticipated.

A few minutes after we got to the classroom, a damp-looking Rani and Maddy were ushered in by a tight-lipped Mrs McGuy. I have to say neither of them was looking their best. Mrs McG disappeared again, gone to fetch her knuckledusters by the look of her.

'She wouldn't even let me blow-dry my hair,' Rani wailed as we got our books together for the first lesson. 'I swear to God she has never gone into the shower room before school the whole time I've been here. She must be able to *smell* people not being where they should be.' Rani put on her Mrs McGuy voice. 'Well helloo, girls. Did we feel like a wee wash? Dearie, dearie me. I've obviously been labouring under a gross misapprehension. I thought that this was a *schoool*. But nooo, I can see from you two ladies, that what we actually have here is a *health spa*. Where would you be off to now, then? Would it be a session of aromatherapy? A wee facial?'

'Oh dear,' I said. 'That's the end of the running to school idea then.' I was not too upset. It was my turn tomorrow.

But Chloe said that because she lives so close to the school we could run to her house and shower and change there. Her mum wouldn't mind. She leaves early to take Jim to his school anyway. So that's good news.

I needed to make my peace with Jennifer. Her hair was washed and blow-dried in the style she had at the party. Did I see mascara on those eyes? And a pink flush on those cheeks? She looked very pretty. I could see it was not only Nathan taking notice. I took a deep breath and went over. Cara and Susie were already complimenting her on her new look. Even Jet looked up from her endless grooming to take her new appearance in.

'Thanks.' Jennifer turned in my direction. 'Carrie, Chloe and Rani helped me.'

'Well, they did a great job,' Cara said, beaming at me. 'Would you help sort me out before the dance?'

I muttered something about being busy but thanks for asking. Then I got to speak to Jennifer alone. 'I'm so sorry about Friday night. I think I did, maybe, give you the wrong . . .'

'Look, Carrie. I don't want to talk about it. I suppose I do have to thank you for helping me get ready. Shame about the rest of the evening. I can't understand what went wrong. I did look absolutely fantastic.'

'That's so true,' I shrieked. 'You looked lovely. But you always were. We just helped bring it out.'

She sniffed. 'I think I would have eventually managed it on my own, you know.' Then she gave me a patronising look.

Well! Not if past attempts were anything to go by, I thought. But I let this comment pass.

'I like to think I helped you out too on Friday,' she continued.

'Really?'

'Yes. I think I stopped someone from wasting their time on you.'

Hmmm.

'Well, if you mean what you said to Jack Harper there was no need. You got that situation completely wrong. He's not the *slightest* bit interested in me like that. Nor me in him.'

'Glad to hear it. I'll pass on the message.' Sasha was standing right beside me. Where had *she* come from? She must have been surprised by my horrified expression because she said quickly, 'Only kidding, Carrie. Course I know you're not interested in Jack. Everyone knows you're with Chris Jones.'

She said this rather too loudly because Jet looked up from filing her nails and smirked. 'That's right you *are, aren't* you?' she said. 'When are you seeing him again?'

'Today,' I snapped and her face fell a bit.

'Well, good luck,' she purred. 'He's a tricky boy to hold on to. You need to keep him on a tight rein . . .'

Mrs McGuy swooped back in and started the register so that was the end of the exchange, but Jet's comments disturbed me. They made me feel worse about telling Chris the bad news.

As I was going into lunch he came over and gave me a huge kiss. In front of everyone. He pulled me over to the side of the dining hall.

My stomach was churning.

'Looking forward to seeing you tonight . . .' he murmured, in full Love Pants mode.

'About this evening,' I interrupted.

'Yeah, like I said, I'm looking forward to it. Come round about eight-thirty. My parents will have gone by then.'

I took a deep breath. 'Chris, I'm sorry but I can't come over. My parents won't let me out that late in the week.' The shame of it.

His face clouded. 'You sure?'

'How do you mean?'

'Couldn't you get out somehow? Say you're going over to a friend's?'

I felt confused now. He was making me feel as if I'd been very stupid. 'I don't know,' I flustered. 'I'll have to think about it. It's kind of short notice.'

'Text me when you've sorted it.' He winked, and did the pointy, clicking finger thing before disappearing.

At lunch break, Rani and Chloe came with me behind the gym for an emergency meeting.

'You can't go,' Chloe said flatly. 'It's wrong of him to ask you to sneak about like that.'

'And you know what will happen if you go to his house,' Rani said darkly.

'What?' I asked.

'Well, groping and hands up the jumper stuff and that's just for starters,' she told me.

'But if I don't go he'll think I'm really pathetic and finish with me. He could go out with anyone,' I said.

Again with the murmurs.

I sighed. '*Apart* from you two. He says I need to try to find a way to get out. He's really looking forward to it.'

'I'll bet he is!' yelped Rani.

'Look. I don't want to lose him. I've only snogged him once and that was under strained circumstances. I need to have another go. If I'm going to be his girlfriend I've got to act mature.'

'It's not acting mature asking you to lie on your first date. And anyway how on earth are you going to get out of the house?' Rani had folded her arms. That's Rani's equivalent of my hand on hips.

I looked sheepishly at them.

'I thought I'd say I needed to come over to your place to get some help with some of my science homework.'

Pursed lips.

'And how would you get over to his house?' Chloe asked.

'On the bus.'

'Are you mad! It's not worth it.'

I was saved from this interrogation by the bell. I thought about it all afternoon (luckily we had double geography – Miss Gooding was back, but her heart was still with Andros the bartender in Ayia Napa) and by the end of the day I had made up my mind.

I could see Chris waiting for me as I walked towards the gates.

Someone grabbed my arm.

'Not so fast, young lady.'

It was Rani.

Rani, Chloe and Maddy bundled me behind the bins.

'Unhand me. I've already made up my mind,' I yelled.

'Carrie, if you go we have decided on a plan. And we really and truly will carry it out,' said Chloe.

'And what plan would that be?'

'You will leave us no choice but to besiege his house,' Rani said gravely.

'Yes, *besiege* it.' Chloe was nodding furiously.

'We will come round and we will be like Cathy in *Wuthering Heights*. We will bang on the windows wailing, "Carrrieeeee, Carrieeeee what are yooo doooing?".'

'I might even take photos,' Maddy added seriously.

'And we've made these to hold up against the windows,' Chloe said.

She held up a piece of paper with: *LEAVE CARRIE ALONE* written on it in fat red felt pen.

Rani lifted, *GET OFF HER – YOU BEAST*.

Maddy pointed solemnly at, *SEE – I'VE GOT A CAMERA*.

But their efforts were wasted. I had already made up my mind what I was going to do.

RANI'S TIP • • • • • • • • • • • • • • • • • • •

To get hair in tip-top condition for a hot date, try this deep conditioning treatment. Rub a little olive oil into your hair, making sure it gets on the ends where your hair is driest. Wrap your head in a warm towel and leave on for an hour or so. Shampoo out. Ask your mum before you do this, because if you use the fancy oil your parents brought back from Italy last year they can get quite stroppy. (Don't ask how I know these things. Just trust me.)

Chapter 18

MY FIRST DATE WITH CHRIS JONES
A faithful recording

We went to The Coffee Bean.

After churning it over all afternoon I made the decision. It didn't make me feel happy. But it made me feel least unhappy.

He wasn't very pleased when I told him but he didn't finish with me or anything like that. So he does like me. Things just went a bit cool for a while.

I asked him lots of questions about the band and about himself generally. He had quite a lot to say about these topics so it kept us going through two coffees. (No chocolate muffins, in spite of being starving – I couldn't risk the high stain factor.) And then he said how much he was looking forward to the dance next weekend. He said how much he'd enjoyed the party and slowly leaned across the table and stroked my hair. And I looked at his blond hair and blue-green eyes and thought he is *so* good looking. And I was wrong to doubt him.

And wait till I tell Rani and Chloe about this.

When I had to go he walked me out of The Coffee Bean and I knew the big kisseroo was coming up. He moved close.

An ear splitting 'Yoo hoo!' ripped through the air.

It was Jet and Melanie.

Crap.

'Hi, Chris.' Jet smirked and flicked a dyed-blond streak. 'Leaving already?'

He seemed indecisive and then said, 'Got ten minutes before I have to go. Be inside in a minute.' And Jet and Melanie walked past us into the café. I could see Jet staring at us through the glass.

And then Chris moved in for the grand finale which was nice but of course it had been spoiled. Yet again!

Please God, can I have just one kiss where I'm not thinking about anything else but only how blissfully lovely it is? Just one kiss which is Wow, Wow, Wow all the way through.

Is it too much to ask?

But he has asked me to the dance (as good as) so I think I can safely assume that we are now officially *going out*.

Which is exciting.

I almost forgot to mention, while we were in the café I saw Jack and Sasha walking past the window together.

So love seems to be in the air.

So that was my first date with Chris Jones. I can't help feeling disappointed about today. Maybe it was just because the kiss was ruined. I thought I'd want to write loads and loads about the date but I don't know why, I'm just not in the mood right now. Maybe I'm getting a bug or something . . .

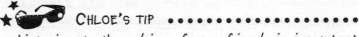

CHLOE'S TIP

Listening to the advice of your friends is important. When shopping for clothes make a pact that you will be honest with each other. You don't have to be mean, a 'No, that's not quite your style' will do. Sometimes you need other people to give you some advice and tell you what your bum really looks like in those jeans. We all want our friends to look great so let them help you.

Chapter 19

Tuesday 5.30 p.m.

This day ended as one of the worst in my life.

And it didn't start too well either.

I was cool with Mum in the car on the way to Maddy's. I didn't want her thinking she'd been right about not letting me go to Chris's house, or anything. Maddy and I had arranged to meet where she'd met Rani, in Pitsford Lane. Rani had been rather vague about how their run had gone. I'd asked Maddy if I should come and pick her up at her house but she got quite agitated about it, so I didn't push it.

This is what I had imagined our run would be like: Me, gazelle-like in the sunshine, hair flowing behind me in the wind, gently encouraging Maddy along the country lanes, thinking about what I would wear for the dance.

What I had not imagined: Me clinging on to a lamp-post with a face the colour of a baboon's bottom, fighting for *my very life*. Breathing is so essential.

Maddy was quite concerned. By the time I got to Chloe's I was nearly a dead person. Maddy was hardly out of puff. I was beginning to suspect why Rani had not said a lot about her turn.

So that was unexpected.

And the next unexpected thing was that while Maddy was in the shower and I was having a restorative cup of tea in the kitchen, Chloe said she needed to talk to me about something serious. This was most unusual. It's always *us* needing to talk to *her*.

She blushed. 'It's Tom. He's started to act so strangely. There's something going on. I just don't know what it is but he's acting differently. And the more I ask him about it the more withdrawn he becomes.'

'Ooooh, don't you worry about that,' I said comfortingly. 'I'm sure you're imagining it.'

She bit her lip and gave me an anxious sideways look. 'You don't think he's going off me? We have been going out for ages and maybe he's tired of me.'

'Tired of you! He's crazy about you. He wakes up every morning and can't believe that he's going out with you – the Beauty of Boughton High.'

'Looks aren't everything, Carrie. You can be beautiful and boring you know. Perhaps he's looking for someone more fiery, more . . . zany, more brainy.' She looked at me sheepishly. 'Someone more like Rani.'

'Rani!' I hooted. 'You've got to be kidding. He adores Rani but she would be his nightmare girlfriend from hell. She's too volatile. You are calm and gentle and wise and grown-up. I can't even believe I'm saying this – you *know* he's not interested in anyone else.'

Chloe looked shifty. 'I know, I know, it's just that I've caught them talking together a couple of times this week and they've sprung apart when I've come up as if they don't want me to know what they're talking about . . .'

When his dad can come and fix the electrics in your attic, I thought. But I said, 'Honestly, Chloe, relax. The one thing I know for one hundred per cent sure is that Tom is *not* going off you.'

And that seemed to cheer her up.

Then she clapped her hand over her mouth. 'What am I thinking of, going on about myself when you had your date with Chris last night! How did it go? Did you get the snog of your dreams at last?'

'Not quite.' And I told her about Jet and Melanie turning up at the wrong moment but how we were definitely officially going out now. I also told her that we should be keeping our eyes on Rani and Kenny too. At last Kenny's attentions had meant she had ditched her hopeless earlier passion for Jonny Poynton. A girl can only sustain unrequited lust for so long. We couldn't walk down any corridor now without Kenny 'just happening' to be there.

Later, at school, I told Rani it had not escaped our notice that she was allowing Kenny to speak to her for longer periods. I think his cheerful refusal to be rebuffed by her was beginning to impress.

Everyone seemed to be talking about the dance this morning. Tess was yelling out over the classroom, 'Who are you going with?' to everyone. She's going with Wayne's brother, Doug Brennan, so God help her.

She asked Sasha if she was going with anyone and Sasha grinned and said maybe.

When I said I was going with Chris Jones a big 'Oooh!' went up.

'Lucky you,' Cara sighed. There was a general feeling of envy and admiration coming my way, which was very enjoyable. Jet was unusually quiet. I wondered if she was at all jealous. I remembered her face when she saw me with Chris at the end of the party. So I tried to be sensitive and not to talk about it too loudly when I was answering the clamour of questions.

Gradually as the day went on I got the feeling that something was up. I felt like Chloe must have done when she surprised Tom and Rani talking about the electrics. People were talking about *me*. By lunchtime I knew that, whatever it was, Tom and Jack knew. Jack and I usually don't have a lot to say to each other these days, but today he seemed to be making an effort to be nice. Tom just looked uncomfortable and nothing *ever* fazes him, until Chloe said, 'What *is* up with you today?' and he said he needed to speak to her. In private. And they left the table.

'Well what the hell is that all about?' I asked.

Rani said cheerfully, 'At least I know it's not about me. Since you told me about Chloe's worries, I haven't spoken a word to Tom.'

'I *know*. And Chloe's finding that even more suspicious.'

Maddy looked uncomfortable and said she needed to go. She had joined the Photography Club.

'It's something about me, isn't it?' I asked her as she got up.

She blushed deep red. 'I've got to go . . . see you,' she said. And she shot off.

'Rani, please go after her and talk to her. Find out what's going on,' I pleaded.

She started to protest and pointed at her half-eaten sandwich but saw my face and went after Maddy. Which left Jack and me at the table.

'Look, I've got to go to band practice now,' he said to me. I knew that. Chris would be there already. He got up next to me and as he did he put his hand on my shoulder and brought his face down close to mine. He said quietly, 'Look . . . Carrie. For what it's worth, I think he's an idiot.'

And I felt rather flushed and got a very bad feeling indeed. Both at the same time. Which was confusing.

I found out what was going on just before afternoon lessons. Rani, Chloe and Maddy reappeared together and said *we all needed to talk*.

We went to the locker room.

Chloe spoke first. 'Carrie, I can't say this so that it won't be painful and just for the record I always thought he was a creep, but last night, after you left The Coffee Bean, Jet left with Chris. She went back to his place and got off with him! She's been telling everyone about it.'

I felt I was falling down a lift shaft. She had let me go on and on about it all morning, knowing that I was making a total fool of myself. So typical of me. Why do I have to blab to the whole world about everything? I am the doggiest-dog person that ever lived.

I felt injected with icy humiliation and I wanted to cry but I couldn't because everyone would know why. Total shame. So I took a deep breath instead and said, 'He's welcome to her. From the way they both behaved they deserve each other.'

Chloe gave me a 'That's the spirit' hug.

Rani looked uncomfortable. 'And Maddy didn't want to tell you but there's something else. On the night of the party before Maddy, er, felt ill, she went outside by herself to get some fresh air and saw Chris kissing Jet in the garden.'

'I think Jack must have seen them too,' Maddy added. 'I think that's why he thought he might have a chance with you.'

I wish she'd stop going on about that.

'But why wasn't Jet mad with Chris that night? Why didn't she say anything then?'

'Well, you wouldn't want to admit that someone had kissed you and then they'd gone off with someone else the same night, would you?' said Rani.

I gave her a long look. She screwed her face up and said, 'Bugger. Sorry, Carrie.'

'Thank you, Rani. But why did he even bother with me? Why didn't he just go out with her right from the start?'

'Because he thinks you're gorgeous and clever but he's a prat about girls. Jet is just so available and he's such a weak, vain idiot.'

For a person who is not angry by nature I was getting very angry now.

In the afternoon I ignored Jet totally. Chloe, Rani, Maddy and I walked coolly past and then had lots of conversations punctuated by tinkling laughter. It didn't make me feel any better. Jet continued to look triumphant.

At last the day was over and I was at the bus stop. Then Chris Jones sauntered over. Rani and Maddy looked anxiously at me.

'You get on the bus,' I said. 'I can handle this.' They got on. I could see their faces pressed against the glass.

'Carrie, can I talk to you?'

'I've nothing to say to you,' I replied icily, doing something very busily with my bag.

'Look, Carrie, I'm sorry; you've got it all wrong. Completely wrong. I've heard what you've been told. Jet's lying. Nothing happened last night. We're just friends. Come on, you've got to believe me. You're the one I want to be with.'

I said nothing.

He bent down and his blond hair flopped over his face and then he looked up into my face and gave me his cutest smile.

'Come on, Carrie, I think you're so great. Forget about Jet. It's you I want to go out with. Honestly. She means nothing to me.'

I looked up and saw that Jet was watching us from the bus. He didn't see her.

'Come on, Carrie, what do you say? Don't be mad at me. Give me a little sign that might give me some hope.'

I looked deep into his blue-green eyes. They really were the most amazing colour.

He was doing his most devastating grin now. He put his head on one side. 'Just one little sign. Pretty please?'

So I slugged him over the back of the head with my school bag.

'That a clear enough sign for you?' I asked. Then I got on the bus.

Tuesday 8.30 p.m.

Mum has just brought me soup and a chicken sandwich. (I am too distressed to go downstairs.) 'Cheer up,' she said. 'There are plenty more fish in the sea, Carrie. And you've got the dance to look forward to.'

I wish I hadn't told her about Chris now – but when the Mum-radar picks up distress, resistance is useless.

I will not be going to the dance. Everyone is either:

1) *Laughing at me.*
2) *Feeling sorry for me.*
3) *Doing both of these at the same time.*

I would rather poke out my eye with a sharp twig than go. I am going to stay in my room till I am eighteen and my youth is over. I'm just going to sit here very still.

Tuesday 8.45 p.m.

Rani has just phoned. She has been to self-defence where Cara told her that Jet was sounding off to everyone who would listen that she is confident that she will be going to the dance with Chris. Apparently she was saying there was no way that I'd dare to show my face there now that I had physically assaulted him in front of witnesses. And now that I had been made such a fool of. She said she didn't really see how I could go on my own. In fact she'd be amazed if I even turned up for school tomorrow.

A gauntlet had been thrown down.

I would not be crushed by that Nancy No-Brain.

I then phoned Rani straight back and said did she mind cancelling her run with Maddy as it would be nice if she was on the bus tomorrow.

She said she'd done it already.

★ 👓 CARRIE'S TIP ● ● ● ● ● ● ● ● ● ● ● ● ● ● ● ● ● ●

Immortalise your friends in a work of art. They deserve it! Dig out the best photos you've got (or get some done in a photo-booth). Then blow them up on a photocopier (Post Offices and stationery shops have them if you can't get access to one anywhere else). Keep blowing up the photo until it's the size you want. The black and white effect is really cool and you can then either leave them as they are, or colour them in yourself. They look great in a row on the wall in cheap clip frames.

Chapter 20

Wednesday 8.15 a.m.

I am on the bus. Jet did not look pleased when I got on. She whispered something to Melanie as I went past. I gave her a glacial look. She looked even less pleased when I said loudly to Rani that I was looking forward to the dance.

It will take a better girl than her to crush the spirit of Carrie Henderson.

Rani has just jogged me by putting both her arms in the air and shouting 'You go girl!' very loudly.

She's not even pretending not to read this any more.

I am glad you are on the bus, Rani.

Do you think you will let Kenny kiss you at the dance?

She has gone red, red, red as a beetroot.

Yes, you have.

Do you think you will let him pull you into his manly arms and press you to his ruby lips?

She has got the giggles now.

Will you waggle your tongue in his mouth?

That was a very loud screech. Does Kenny like screeching then?

See how I'm bringing laughter to others in spite of my pain.

Wednesday 8.25 a.m.

Maddy just got on. She asked us if we wanted to go running back to Pitsford after school. We both said quickly that we didn't have our running clothes but Maddy pointed out that we could just wear our gym stuff. In public?! Day-Glo Aertex blouse and navy divided skirt? I so don't think so. But then I felt bad as I know how much the running means to her and she looks so much healthier already . . . And it's because of me that she missed it this morning.

So I said yes, but I'd compromise and wear my school shirt. Rani said OK too.

What the hell. It's the least of my worries.

I just want to get through the day.

8.00 p.m.

Survived school. But I am exhausted. It has been a crazy day. Maddy was nearly molested on Pitsford Recreation Ground. Then we got to go to her house.

These events have certainly helped *take my mind off things*.

Chris kept well away all day and, although Jet was bitching and simpering every time I turned my back, she kept her distance too. But it wasn't what you'd call fun.

I saw Sasha talking to Jack at break. She's all over him at the moment. Cara said she told her she finds him 'interesting', which is unusual as Sasha's never found any boy anything other than a total pushover. I wasn't going to ask Jack any questions about it. He was being kind at lunch and making me laugh. Which helped take my mind off things too.

Rani was giving out final details of the room makeover to everyone. (I'm on sari curtains, cushions and bedspreads with her.) Tom left his to-do list on the table and she had to run after him. I watched in horror as Chloe, returning from an extra flute lesson, came up behind them. Tom stuffed the note into his pocket but I could see that Chloe had noticed. Then I watched in agony as Rani and Tom hopped from foot to foot making up some rubbish. It is such bad luck that those two are the worst liars in the world.

Rani said proudly that she had told Chloe Tom wanted to join self-defence and she was giving him the number of her teacher.

Brilliant. Positively inspired. The biggest, strongest boy in school. Sooo likely he's going to join self-defence.

Anyway, about saving Maddy from molestation.

As we panted across Pitsford recreation ground (Yahoo! As I suspected: Rani was a rubbish runner too, Maddy was miles ahead of both of us) Wayne Brennan, who had been watching her come along the path, blocked her way.

By the time we caught up with her Wayne was in full conversational flow. He had a beer can in one hand and from the state of him it wasn't his first of the day. 'Look! It's my party girl. How's it going?' He put his arm over her shoulders. Maddy tried to shake him off but he didn't take his arm away. He is very big. He breathed, 'Hope you're feeling a little better now,' into her face. She winced.

'Leave her alone,' I shouted.

'No, no, no. You don't get it. Your friend here likes to party, don't you?' he said, as he lifted the can up towards her face.

'Just let her go,' I warned him.

'Or what?'

'Or my friend here,' I pointed to Rani, looking very tiny in her gym kit, 'well . . . she does self-defence. She has moves. Her hands are deadly weapons.'

While his quick brain was absorbing that information Rani tugged at my shirt and said could she have a quick word. I felt it wasn't the best time but we retreated a few steps. 'What the hell are you saying!' she blurted out.

'I'm *saying* that you are a self-defence expert. Why don't you sort him out with a few of your jabs and pokes and stuff?'

'I've only just started! I'm not ready for Wayne Brennan.'

I was disappointed with this news. And a little unsure what to do next. Luckily Maddy wasn't. As he started grabbing at her again, she scraped her foot down his shin, stamped hard on his toe and yelled, 'Run! Run!'

So we did. (OK. We didn't really save her but we would have done if we'd had to.)

We ran to Pitsford Lane. Then we had to stop, as I don't know why, but we were all laughing so much we couldn't go any further.

When Maddy was capable of speech she asked, 'Do you want to come to my place for a Coke or something?'

We said we would and felt good about it. At last she trusted us enough to know that we didn't care where she lived.

The next bit is so major I need to get a bowl of cereal and a hot chocolate to sustain me before I put it down on paper. Dr Jennings will fall off her chair.

 RANI'S TIP ●

To get lips looking as good as they can for possible future kissing: Avoid dark lipstick colours if you have thin lips. A shiny, lighter shade will make them look bigger. Put your lip liner just outside your natural lip line.

If you have big lips that you want to look smaller, put the liner just inside your natural lip line, using a light shade, then fill with a deeper, but still lightish lip colour.

Chapter 21

MY VISIT TO MADDY'S HOUSE

My first inkling that I might have made a mistake about where Maddy lived was when she went up to these huge steel gates behind us in the lane and pressed the intercom. She spoke into the machine. There was an electronic whirr of a camera overhead and the gates swung open.

We walked down this huge driveway. The house was hidden by tall trees.

'You live *here*?' I said. Rani was giving me a special look.

'Well . . . yes.' Maddy looked at me as if I was a bit thick.

'I know, I just thought that you lived . . . somewhere else.'

'Like *where*?' Maddy now was certain I was a cretin.

'Like, um, in the flats at the other end of the lane.'

'What?! The derelict flats?' She was laughing. 'No, It's a neat place to photograph and I've been there in the early morning lately to take pictures but no one lives there!'

'No one lives there,' Rani mouthed at me.

Then the house came into view. Not so much a house. More of a sculpture. A sculpture of smooth white rectangles and glittering glass walls, three storeys high. In front of it lay a long, narrow, pale green pool. You reached the front door by crossing a thick sheet of greeny glass suspended above the water.

A man in a dark suit came and slid the glass panel aside to let us in. Maddy spoke briefly to him and he disappeared again.

'Is that your dad?' Rani asked.

Maddy smiled and said, 'No that was Mr Hunt. He, um, helps out around the place.'

'In a suit?'

'Well, he doesn't do outdoor stuff.'

'He's like your butler, isn't he?' I said. (I should be a detective.) But then we were inside and I was too overwhelmed to speak.

It was the most amazing house I'd ever been in. It was like in a magazine.

Rani couldn't resist and kicked off her shoes and leaped on to the enormous white sofa and started doing snow angel movements.

'Hello, girls.' Maddy's mum came in. Not looking harassed today and wearing a simple black silk top and trousers that just screamed designer. Rani jumped off the sofa but Maddy's mum simply smiled and said how glad she was that Maddy had settled into Boughton so well and thanked us for going running with her. She also asked if perhaps we'd like to see the rest of the house and that Maddy should take us round.

Yes, please.

I had fallen in love with the huge light space, the pale stone floors and the smooth lines of the furniture. Everything looked like a work of art. Then I noticed a group of black and white photos on one wall.

'That's the designer Trudi Hill, isn't it? And isn't that Mei Mei, the Chinese supermodel?'

And then I noticed that on the thick slab of black stone that served for a coffee table there was the biggest pile of fashion magazines I'd ever seen. Chloe would be in heaven.

This woman was obviously seriously into style.

Maddy took us on a tour of one room after another. Living in her house must be like staying in the poshest hotel. *All the time.*

'You could play football in some of these rooms – they're huge!' Rani gasped.

Then we got to Maddy's room.

I had to smile because although it had the same pale floors and walls as the others it definitely had Maddy's stamp on it. Posters of her favourite bands were stuck up crooked everywhere and piles of papers, CDs, magazines and photographs lay around tidied into tottering piles.

She pointed out her dark room where she developed her photos. She had an amazing limestone bathroom all to herself. With big fluffy towels. Not like the bathroom I have to share with Ned. Where were the gungy shampoo bottle, a topless toothpaste tube and the soggy towel on the floor?

The best bit of all was her walk-in wardrobe. I couldn't resist asking Maddy if I could open one of the cupboards. I was curious, as I've only ever seen her wear about three things apart from school uniform.

Well, my jaw dropped with shock. Her cupboards were full of designer clothes. Rack after rack of Armani and Versace and just about anyone else you'd ever heard of.

'Why don't you wear these clothes?' I gasped.

Maddy looked embarrassed.

'Well, I can't fit into a lot of them and it's not my style to dress up.'

'But how come you *have* them?'

But before she could answer Rani's attention had been caught by a box on the dressing table. It was covered in thick cream paper and had an expensive black silk ribbon tied loosely around it.

'That's a Carlo Cerranti box, isn't it?'

'Yes, it's for Chloe. I was going to give it to her on her birthday.' Maddy hesitated. 'Do you want to see?'

Oh yes. I think we did.

Inside, nestling in layers of tissue paper lay the most beautiful soft suede boots I had ever seen. They were pale cream and when I touched one it was like stroking a rose petal.

They were the ones that Chloe had seen in *Vogue*.

'They must have cost hundreds and hundreds and *hundreds . . .*'

Maddy blushed. 'Well, I hope she likes them. I felt so bad about ruining her other ones.'

'What is going on here, Maddy?' I asked. 'You have cupboards full of designer clothes and you have boots that cost the earth.'

'I know, I know, but it's not quite what you think. We get sent it. Loads of stuff, from designers. It's part of what my dad does.'

'Your dad!' I shrieked. (Well, I *was* having a very surprising time.)

Then Rani shrieked and waved a photo around she'd picked up off the dressing table. 'Oh my God! Please don't tell me that this is your dad.' She was looking at a photo of a tall man in a black suit and cowboy hat.

Maddy blushed again.

'It's him, isn't it?' asked Rani. 'It's Daniel Van de Velde!'

Maddy managed a smile. 'Yeah, that's him. I tend not to use my full surname – it's too long. My dad works in the fashion world. That's why we get all the freebies from designers. It's normal in his line of work And that's why a lot of it doesn't fit me. Models are kind of teeny.'

'He *is* the fashion world! He's the most influential and famous journalist in the business. Wait till Chloe hears about this. He's her idol.'

And then I got overexcited and pulled things out of the cupboard saying, 'Maddy, Maddy, you can wear loads of this stuff. Let's do a makeover on you before the dance on Saturday.'

Rani was nodding enthusiastically, but Maddy said 'No' very firmly.

'I want to do my own thing. Look. I didn't want to use my dad's name in school because in Beverly Hills people were only ever friendly towards me because of him. They'd be so nice and then as soon as they got home it was obvious that they weren't interested in being my friend at all. It was just until they got to meet my dad. I've always felt that I can't be the pretty, talented daughter my dad wants anyway. I think the way I looked when I first came here was a way of saying I can't be those things so I'll be this other extreme thing instead. But it wasn't me. Now I just want to find what is really right for me. On my own.'

I went to give her a hug and said, 'I wish I was as wise as you.'

And I meant it. Seeing Maddy's house confirmed something I was becoming increasingly aware of. My judgement, that I'd imagined was so good, had been wildly off lately. I had assumed this whole story in my head about Maddy and her life based on a single sighting of her outside some flats one morning. I couldn't have got it more wrong.

Like I got it wrong about matchmaking Jennifer and I got it wrong about what I felt about Chris. And I had got it seriously wrong about what I felt about someone else and now it was too late and it was all my fault.

★ CHLOE'S TIP ●●●●●●●●●●●●●●●●●●●●

Don't let hours of preparation time go to waste by putting a great outfit over the wrong underwear. There's nothing grottier than a grubby bra strap on show. Also Visible Panty Line makes your bum look bigger. Avoid it if you can with careful choice of knickers.

Chapter 22

I did not write in this diary yesterday. I was too busy surviving school. To be honest, I'm too depressed to write much today. I had to stay behind to get the decorations organised for the dance on Saturday. As well as pinning up painted sheets and tying on fake foliage, I had to untangle about a hundred strings of fairy lights. I had asked everyone I knew to search them out of their Christmas decorations. I was determined to give it my best effort and get the hall looking really good – I didn't want to give Jet something else to crow over if I got it wrong.

Also, Mum decided to wrap Gran's present. Absence of expensive wrapping paper immediately spotted. She made me iron for an hour. I live in a dictatorship.

Today I did these things:

1) *Sewed cushions, bedcovers and curtains at Rani's this evening. My fingers are pincushions. Her mum watched us struggle for ages, making our tiny stitches, before she put us out of our misery and finished them off on her sewing machine. She said we were a disgrace to child labour and would have starved to death in Victorian times. She and Mum are taking everything over to Chloe's tomorrow morning and storing it in the attic. Chloe is going to be out with Jim. Mum has bought her a beautiful little antique mirror and Rani's mum is bringing two Indian pierced metal lanterns. It's*

going to be so lovely. The plan is that we all go over on Sunday, her birthday. Her dad is taking her out for the day and when he brings her back the electricity will work, the room will be sorted and Ta Da – surprise!

2) *Told Chloe about our visit to Maddy's (not the boots bit of course). She nearly fainted. She will never give up on her dream to be a fashion journalist. She needs cheering up because she's still feeling funny about Tom. And she's being cool-ish with Rani, which is totally unlike her. I will be glad when this secret is out because I don't think the poor girl can stand much more. Tom and Rani are pretty miserable about it too. Not a good atmosphere at lunch. Though Jack tried his best to cheer things along. Even though I'm putting a brave face on it – I am dreading the dance.*

3) *Told Rani, Chloe and Maddy that I am not looking forward to the dance.*

They said, 'We know.'

And I said, 'You don't understand, you think it's about Chris Jones, but it's not.'

And they said, 'We know.'

And I explained that the only feeling I had about Chris was embarrassment that he had made a fool of me. I had no regrets about not seeing him again. He was kind of boring. And vain. And self-obsessed.

And they said, 'We know.'

'I must have been mad to have fallen for that fake charm,' I admitted.

They didn't say 'We know', but said best-friend-soothing things. But all the comforting words in the world couldn't change the real reason why I don't want to go to the dance. Which I can't write down because it will show that I am the stupidest girl in stupid town who has just graduated from stupid university.

With honours.

★ CARRIE'S TIP ●●●●●●●●●●●●●●●●●●●●
Accessorise a room with cushions, mirrors, pictures, etc. Revamp old cushions and duvet covers by cutting shapes out of washable material and sticking or sewing them on. You could do flowers, letters or a geometric design. Let your creative side go wild.

Chapter 23

Saturday 10.00 a.m.

Only nine and a half hours to get ready for the dance. I have decided I will make an effort anyway. Even if it is only to show Jet that my spirit is not broken. Though I think my heart is. When you realise you really, really like a dark, intense, poet-type person and you know you are going to have to spend a whole evening watching them with someone else, it's not a good feeling.

Right. Anything else that could make it worse?

I have forgotten to tell Mum she must not dance. I will go down and do so now.

Saturday 10.15 a.m.

I don't know what is the matter with her. She has no consideration for my feelings. She laughed. She has no intention of not dancing. I must phone Rani.

Saturday 10.25 a.m.

Rani said she sympathised. Her father actually did a John Travolta impression at the last party they had at their house and has threatened to do it again when he comes to pick her up tonight. She has been in tears.

Saturday 10.40 a.m.

I have just phoned Chloe. She says she wouldn't mind if her mum was the worst dancer in the world (sorry, Chloe – that title is already taken by mine), she would just be glad to see her having a good time. She wishes her mum had a dance to go to. She is the kindest girl in the world. If that's not self-sacrifice I don't know what is.

She is going to bring a pile of clothes and accessories with her this afternoon. Rani is bringing make-up and hair styling equipment. Maddy is going to meet us there and has been very mysterious about what she's going to wear. 'You'll see me at the dance,' is all she said at school yesterday.

Saturday 6.30 p.m.

We are all ready. Dad has just insisted on taking a photo of all of us on the stairs with Mum. She is in an orange dress that will be useful if we get shipwrecked and need to attract the attention of passing boats.

As for me, the spinster (again) of this parish, I am in a pale green floaty mini. It has bootlace straps and I'm wearing it with a necklace of pale yellow and green glass flowers that Chloe lent me. Rani has tied a thin green ribbon through a few small plaits and tied them together loosely at the back. Rani has done my eyes with a grey-green shadow and I'm wearing a pinky-beige lipstick. Chloe said I look like a wood nymph and Chris will be devastated he won't be with me. Which is a lie of course. I know they are just trying to cheer me up. I expect Jet has been practising her triumphant sneers in the mirror. The irony is that she won't believe I'm not heartbroken. I suppose it's been obvious to everyone that I've been low these past few days. Even Sasha came up and said, 'Sometimes these things aren't meant to be. Perhaps your stars were saying you weren't in the right time and place for each other.' Now that *is* irony. I think Dr Jennings would agree.

Thank goodness for my friends. Rani is looking at me anxiously, smoothing down an orange silky top and a cream skirt, dotted with tiny brown sequins. She has less make-up on than usual and looks fresh and sparkly.

'I'm fed up with trying to look older,' she said. 'I just want to look in the mirror and see myself.'

Kenny Lee will be bowled over. He already thinks she's the most exotic flower that ever trod the earth.

We are ready to go.

Sunday 2.00 a.m.!!
Well.

It was one of those nights you are going to want to remember for the rest of your life. Even the painful bits.

Yes, Dr J, get your pen poised to take notes.

First good thing was that all our hard work on the hall had paid off. White roses wound themselves around the pillars. Dainty paper lanterns hung from ivy garlands strung between them. We had painted silver moons and stars on to dark blue canopies and arches of fairy lights were draped over the doors and windows.

Daniel Van de Velde was there! Maddy said he was arriving this afternoon and had promised to drive her to the dance. He was causing quite a stir, chatting to *my* mum and managing not to look directly into the orange for fear of going blind.

Next good thing was, as he turned to leave, the attractive brunette standing next to him waved at us and came over. Maddy! We all just gawped. She looked fantastic! We saw now she had been right not to let us interfere. We wouldn't have been able to do better. Her dark hair had been cut into a thick, smooth bob. A sharp fringe fell from the dark red silk band tied into her hair. Her skin glowed. She was wearing a three-quarter length black Versace coat over dark red, heavy silk trousers, her eyes were lightly smudged with dark grey and her lips were a shiny plum colour. It was hard to recognise the girl from Barnaby's.

'Wow!' Chloe gasped. 'You look fabulous!'

Maddy blushed and said thanks. Then Tom, Kenny and Jack arrived and Tom said we *all* looked fabulous and reached out to swing Chloe off to the dance floor. Chloe was wearing a vintage red taffeta dress that she got in a second-hand shop. It was strapless with a circular skirt that flared out and would show her knickers if she twirled round and round (which she wanted me to say she *wouldn't* be doing – but then she did a bit). She was wearing red lipstick that matched and had got some fabulous artificial black roses in her hair. It looked great with her pale skin, green eyes and dark curly hair. She grabbed Tom's hand and seemed determined to forget about her worries about him.

Kenny then asked Rani to dance but she obviously couldn't resist one last stab at playing hard to get and said, 'Not just now, maybe later.'

Kenny looked her straight in the eye. 'OK, I get the message,' he said, deliberately. 'I'm going to go now.' And he began to move away. 'And I may not be back.' He said over his shoulder.

He went a few yards further. Then turned around again. 'I'm serious you know. That could have been your last chance.'

Rani began to look anxious.

He got halfway across and cupped his hands to his mouth. 'I'LL BE OFF NOW THEN.'

We watched his retreating back.

'DID YOU GET THAT?' He yelled from the across the hall. 'I'LL SAY GOODBYE NOW.'

Rani began to laugh as we watched him make a big mega-phone out of one of the posters for the dance and started climbing a pillar.

'For God's sake, put that boy out of his misery and go and dance with him,' I said. 'You know you want to.'

So she did.

Then Joe Carter came up and asked Maddy to dance.

Which just left Jack and me.

'Got anyone lined up for me this evening, then?' he asked, smiling at me with those dark eyes.

'NO!' I squeaked. 'No. No, that was a huge mistake. My matchmaking days are long over. Anyway you're with . . . Wow!'

I was distracted by the arrival of Jennifer who had taken every tip we had given her and put it to good use. With her shiny fair hair, little blue satin dress and silver strappy heels she looked very cute indeed.

'See,' I couldn't stop myself saying. 'She *is* so pretty. And she thought you were gorgeous.'

'Unlike some people.' He raised an eyebrow at me.

I took a deep breath.

'Listen, Jack. About what I said to Jennifer. I didn't mean those things. I only said them to her to make her feel better about it not working out between you.'

'I still don't know what made you think they would.'

'Well, she's pretty and you weren't going out with anyone . . .'

'No, I wasn't, was I? I wonder why that might have been?'

'Well,' He was standing very close now. 'I . . . er, don't know.'

'Perhaps it's because I'm *way* too intense?'

'No! I don't think you are, not at all. Well, you can be at times, but in a good way, a good, good way.' (Oh dear, was this all going horribly wrong?) 'I'm personally a big fan of your intensity.'

God did I really say that?

He was laughing now. 'You can't help yourself, Carrie, can you? And what about the not-at-all-good-looking part?'

I pulled a face. 'We-ell, let's not go mad. And anyway you can't be too hideous or else . . .'

'Or else what?'

'Or else a girl like Sasha wouldn't go out with you,' I said firmly, as I spotted her walking towards us. 'Got to go now, bye.'

And that was painful. Made worse by Jet, glittering like a second-hand car showroom, walking by and saying, 'All alone, Carrie?' as she headed over to where Chris was hanging out.

Then disasters started clattering down like dominoes.

I was talking to Maddy and Joe later when Rani bounced up to tell me she had news from Tom. His dad couldn't do the electrics tomorrow. He had an emergency job on. We weren't to worry though because it would be daylight when Chloe got back from her dad's and saw the room for the first time. He was going to do it on Monday. She was to pass this message on to everyone involved.

An anxious feeling crept over me. 'How did Tom manage to tell you all that? He's been with Chloe all evening.'

'Have no fear, Carrie, my dear. He *très*, *très* discreetly passed this on to me when Chloe was getting a drink.' And she waved a piece of paper in the air.

'*What's in that note?!*' Chloe had suddenly appeared at our side.

Rani closed her fingers around it and clutched it to her chest. 'Nothing.'

'Give me that note.'

Rani looked agonised. 'I can't,' she said.

'Why not? Look, I just *saw* Tom give it to you. And it's not the first time it's happened. I want to know what's going on. *Give me the note.*'

She was grabbing for it now.

Rani did the only thing Rani would do in the circumstances. She stuffed the paper into her mouth and starting chewing, looked like she was going to be sick, and ran.

Chloe looked angrily at me. 'You know about this, don't you? You know that there is something going on between Tom and Rani and you haven't told me. Am I the only person who doesn't know? For God's sake . . .' She burst into tears. 'You're my *best friends*.' And she ran out of the hall.

This was a catastrophe. I told Maddy to go and get Tom and I went after her. It was freezing outside and I couldn't see her anywhere. I did meet Jack though.

'I've been looking for you,' he said.

'Why?'

'I need to tell you something.'

'Now?' I said desperately. 'It's not really a good time, Jack – I'm looking for Chloe.'

'It won't take long,' he said, moving closer.

'I'm sorry, Jack, I've really got to go. Tom wrote Rani a note and . . .'

'I'm not going out with Sasha any more,' he blurted. 'It just didn't work. It never really started.'

My heart began to beat very fast.

'The problem is,' he paused. 'The problem is, I've only ever been interested in one girl since I started at Boughton. And no one else will do . . . And she is a *very* hard girl to pin down.'

He was standing *very* close now.

'I'm hoping my timing will be better tonight than it has been in the past.'

Every fibre in my being wanted to stay and listen to some more of this conversation but I knew that Chloe was out there somewhere feeling wretched. And what had I said? Friends first.

'Jack, I really, really want to talk but . . .'

His face fell.

'Bad timing again?'

And I winced and nodded and said I'd explain later, leaving him leaning against the gym wall. He called quietly after me.

'Don't worry, Carrie, I think I've got the message.'

I didn't find Chloe but Tom did. I met him in the car park. Chloe had just told him it was all over between them.

'It nearly killed me not to tell her everything, Carrie. I don't think I can wait until tomorrow.'

And neither did I. Enough was enough. It was nine o'clock. The dance finished in three hours. That would be midnight. It would be Chloe's birthday.

I went back into the hall to find an anxious Rani, Maddy and Kenny wondering what was going on. I briefed them about what I was going to do. I spoke to Mum. She listened carefully, nodded and went to make a call on her mobile.

Then I went to find Jack. He was still outside. My heart went cold when I saw Sasha walking away from him. As she passed me she said, 'I thought it was worth one last try as I really didn't know if you were interested in him, Carrie. Seems like I'm out of luck. Shame, he's pretty cool. Back to the band boys for me.' She gave me a huge grin and sauntered merrily back to the hall. And I looked back at her and I couldn't help smiling too.

Jack looked positively wary as I approached, for which he could not be blamed. 'Jack. I need your help,' I said.

He put his head in his hands and groaned. 'What now?'

And I gently took one of his hands and said I'd tell him on the way. Oh and could he phone his dad and ask him to collect every single candle in his house, and Pitsford Hall is a huge place – there must be loads of them – and bring them to Chloe's flat?

I might just close my eyes for a minute. It's been a long day and I'm not used to being awake at this hour.

 RANI'S TIP ●

Parties are a great excuse for going mad with your make-up. You can wear smokier shadows, brighter colours, even glitter on your cheeks and eyelids if you feel like it. Take a bag of the basics with you to touch up during the evening and some cleansing wipes - when you get hot, your make-up can start to slide. So remember that powder has a greater staying power than creams.

Chapter 24

Sunday 6.00 a.m.

Chloe's face when she walked into the little attic room was just incredible. At first it was amazed and then it just glowed with happiness. We'd lit candles on every surface, put tiny night-lights in big white bowls on the floor and large fat candles flickered in the fireplace.

They illuminated the floating white canopy with tiny silver stars above the bed and the curtain across the window. Large soft pink cushions lay on the white bedspread. The Indian lanterns hung from the beams. Mum's present, the antique mirror, hung above the chest of drawers where I had arranged Chloe's things. A small chair with a pink cushion was tucked under the little desk.

She then went all weepy and soppy and full of apologies for doubting Tom and Rani.

And Rani said, 'No offence but even if he was the last boy on earth . . .'

To which Tom replied, 'Oi! I am in the *room.*'

Then we had hugs all round and told Chloe the whole story.

Maddy's photos had been put up. Six large black and white prints – some of the room at various stages of the makeover and of us just laughing and talking and messing about. She had phoned her dad to collect them, bring them to the dance and then give everyone a lift over to the flat. He was with the other parents downstairs.

'Maddy, these are amazing. Thank you so much.'

Maddy blushed and I thought well, Mr Van de Velde, look at your attractive and talented daughter now.

'Er, I've got something else for you, Chloe.' Maddy held out a cream box tied with black ribbon. 'These are to replace the ones I ruined.'

Chloe looked confused. 'There was no need.'

'Go on then, open it,' Rani urged.

Chloe slowly untied the ribbon and lifted the lid. There were the Cerranti boots we had seen at Maddy's. Their soft, pale suede nestling in the tissue paper. She stared down at them. 'I couldn't, I can't,' she croaked.

'Sure you can, honey,' Maddy said very firmly. 'I owe you.'

Jim looked solemnly on. He had been very surprised when we had arrived earlier and rushed past a smiling Mrs Simmonds towards the attic. He forgave us for not telling him about it after being put in charge of putting the tea lights all over the room. He looked at his sister, puzzled. 'Why is Chloe crying on her new boots?'

And Chloe looked up around the room and said, 'Because I've got the best friends in the world.'

Then we all had to hug again.

I looked at Jack. He grinned back. We had worked so hard we had barely had time to say a word to each other, but it had all been worth it to see Chloe so happy.

I asked Rani if she had had the perfect kiss yet.

She sighed philosophically. 'Well, it was a bit hectic what with one thing and another. Bit too much dashing about and people crying in separate corners – Chloe and me mostly. I think Kenny found the fact I kept sobbing about having messed everything up not very encouraging. He was lovely and kind but the right moment just didn't happen.'

'When is it going to happen then?' I asked.

'Don't worry. He's said we should go to the cinema soon.'

'Oooh careful,' I said. 'No escape then! All dark and cosy in the back seats.'

She gave me a wicked grin and crossed her fingers. 'Ooh,' she said, 'and there's something else you missed, Carrie.'

'What?'

'Guess who was the girl with the sulkiest face of the evening?'

'Who?'

'Jet!' Rani, Maddy and Chloe all chorused together.

'But why? Surely she and Chris . . .?'

'Oh nooooo.' Chloe shook her head. 'Chris found *another* girl to spend the evening with. He hardly spoke to Jet.'

'Go on,' I urged.

'Guess.' Rani clapped her hands together.

'I can't!'

'*Jennifer Cooper!*' they shrieked.

I know this might make me sound like a horrible person but I couldn't help being pleased that Jet and Chris hadn't got together. I had the feeling that Chris and Jennifer might make the perfect couple.

Then Chloe's mum said there was birthday cake downstairs and there was a stampede.

Except for Jack and me. Who found ourselves alone in the candlelit room.

He walked over to me. 'OK, Carrie,' he said, softly. 'I'm going to attempt to do something now that I've been wanting to do for a long time.'

My heart was fluttering like a zillion birds.

'But before I do I'd like you to promise me something.'

'What?'

He began to tick the following off on his fingers. 'You will not suddenly have to agree to go out with another boy, chuck macaroni cheese over someone, find me a girlfriend, tend to the sick, convince yourself I like someone better than you, or look for a distraught friend in the school car park.'

'I won't.'

And then I just *had* to say it. 'Er . . . except for the distraught friend . . . or a sick one, I'd always have to put a distraught friend or sick one first. Or . . . um, any friend that needed me. You do know that.'

God, Carrie, shut up! Thankfully, he was smiling at me.

'I know. That's one of the many things I like about you. Any chance though, that your friends could do without you just for a few minutes?'

I heard the sound of Rani and Chloe's laughing coming up the stairs.

'I think so,' I said.

'So I have your full attention?'

'Yes, you do.'

And he kissed me.

Wow. Wow. Wow.

CARRIE, RANI AND CHLOE'S BEST TIP ••••

Love your friends.

They never go out of style.

www.piccadillypress.co.uk

☆ The latest news on forthcoming books

☆ Chapter previews

☆ Author biographies

☆ Fun quizzes

☆ Reader reviews

☆ Competitions and fab prizes

☆ Book features and cool downloads

☆ And much, much more . . .

Log on and check it out!

Piccadilly Press